EMBRACE
THE WOLF

Leo Haggerty Novels by Benjamin M. Schutz

EMBRACE THE WOLF

Benjamin M. Schutz

BLUEJAY BOOKS INC.

A Bluejay Book, published by arrangement with the Author.

Copyright © 1985 by Benjamin M. Schutz

Jacket art by Jill Bauman

Book design by Terry McCabe

Manufactured in the United States of America

First Bluejay printing: March 1985

Library of Congress Cataloging in Publication Data

This one is for JoAnne:
a comfort and a delight
and the best thing
that ever happened to me.

Acknowledgements

I'd like to thank the following people for the gracious donation of their expertise. The responsibility for the uses to which I put their knowledge is entirely mine. The pseudonymous Ms. Valens at security; Reverend James Mayworm; Mark Schutz, M.D.; Officer Adam Schutz, MCPD; Neil Ruther, attorney-at-law; Chief Wade Pelletier and Officer Margie Young of the Atlantic Beach, North Carolina, Police Department; Captain Franko of the MAKO; Jim Holliday, adult cinema's leading archivist and critic; Meg Hennigan; and Steven Spruill who believed I could write long before there was any reason to.

The heart asks pleasure — first
and then — excuse from pain
and then — those little anodynes
that deaden suffering.

And then to go to sleep
and then if it should be
the will of its inquisitor
the privilege to die.
— Emily Dickinson

EMBRACE
THE WOLF

Chapter 1

HERB SAUNDERS CIRCLED THE PHONE LIKE A DYING ANIMAL DOES a polluted water hole: it can't leave and it can't drink. It had been almost three days since that first phone call. A frozen voice had said, "Mr. Saunders, I have your girls. I think it's time we talked. I'll be in touch." Since then he'd been sitting by the phone. He even shit with the door open so he wouldn't miss a ring. His wife, Maggie, hadn't even commented on that. She'd seen so many of his phases it would take more than that for her to mention it. He was grateful and knew he should thank her. Anyone else would have had him committed by now, or left. She just went on day after day. Those days when he didn't move at all she'd hold him periodically, kiss his forehead, and cradle him in her arms. Back then he truly believed that if he sat perfectly still he would hear the girls' voices or see a vapor trail of their path. He just needed to get still enough. He never could.

The girls had been gone now almost five years. First there had been a sick, spinning anxiety. This can't be. Then ever so briefly "Goddammit, girls. I told you not to go over to Tammy's. To tell your mother where you're going. When you come back, so help me . . ." They never did come back. When it was clear that this was no random accident, no vagrant illness, that someone had done this on purpose, an inexhaustible engine of rage fired up in Herb Saunders. His motor had raced on undiminished since that moment.

There had been nothing for so long. The cranks and nuisance loonies had stopped calling long ago. Life moved on for everyone else. There had been the psychics too. "I see your daughter at a taco stand in San Antonio. Please send five hundred dollars for the address."

For the longest time he wondered how Maggie endured, but he never had the guts to ask her. He was always afraid she'd start to explain and lose it. It would just fly out of her mouth. He'd made it this far by never grieving, never touching that cold lump of sorrow he knew was surely there somewhere. All the therapy with Dr. Prentice hadn't changed a thing. He'd told Prentice that insight wasn't all it was cracked up to be. He knew exactly where he was: the intersection of Hell and Vine. And he knew exactly how he'd gotten there. Someone had taken his life, put it in the shit machine and turned it into garbage. Acceptance was a word he had never learned, and this lesson too was lost on him.

Saunders was getting double vision staring at the phone. Fed up, he screamed, "Call, you son of a bitch, call!" Then softer he said, "Don't do this to me. Not now. Not after all this time." The trace was still on the phone line. It was a Perpetual. The first call had been a local one. The switching station had been identified. If the same line was used, the exact exchange and location could be pinpointed. And then Herb knew they'd talk. Only first he was going to reach down the stranger's throat and rip his tongue out. The coldness of the voice he'd heard had convinced him that this was the man. Who else would remember the number? Catchy as it was: KID-LOST.

Every black hole disgorges itself somewhere into the universe. It's cosmic plumbing: out the black holes and in the white holes. The end of the universe is its beginning. An immense Möbius strip. Herb refused to believe that thermodynamics was going to be revoked just for him. If they left here, they'd have to show up somewhere, someday.

He stood up, stretched his legs, and went to the window. Peeking out he confirmed that suburbia was still there and Maggie was still at work. Well, he thought, somebody had to. He was a hell of a breadwinner. Breadwinner? Not even a crumb-catcher. He couldn't even get it together to get welfare.

The phone rang. He couldn't believe it. He'd conjured up the ring in his mind for so long he thought he was imagining it again. No, it was real. He picked up the phone and put it to his ear. The iceman came on.

"Mr. Saunders?"

"Yes."

"I have someone here who wants to speak with you."

"Tina? Molly?"

A plaintive voice came on. "Daddy?"

"Yes, baby." There was silence. "Baby?"

The phone erupted with a shriek, "Daddy! Help me!"

A scream filled the phone. It went into him like an ice pick in the ear and rose in a wave without crest. The iceman's voice came back on.

"The other one does not speak anymore. Have a good day."

"Tina? Molly? Tina! Molly!"

Nothing. Gone. The end. He slid down the wall to the floor, the dead receiver in his hand.

"Oh my babies, what's happened to you?"

Spastic with horror, his feet were twitching to get him away. The phone fell. He saw trolls, demons, racks, fire, evil hoses, electricity. Eyes kept coming up at him, all with a shrieking soundtrack. Girls. Babies. Children. He could not, would not see their faces. They called out to him. "Do not call my name," he screamed. They cried "help me." He was on all fours, puking a pain he could not disgorge, a nightmare he could not flee. He fell over on his side, panting—an animal dying on the roadway. Still twitching, he wiped his mouth. The phone lay there making its own noisy death rattle. *Get hold of yourself*, he thought. *You stupid shit, don't fold up now. Get moving. React. Act. Do something.*

He got up and slid into the chair. First, a deep breath to calm himself. To do what he knew he needed to, he had to sound calm, controlled, uninvolved. As he dialed the number he wondered, *Why wouldn't the holes sit still?*

"Security Office."

"Yes, this is Sergeant DeVito, on the Saunders' case. You have a trace on that line. We need the number immediately. A child's life is in danger."

"Yes, officer. And your badge number?"

"335. Hurry. Please."

"The line was silent. He prayed, *Don't let him get away. Not again. Not this close.* Thoughts floated up about that Italian kid in the well. The man hanging upside down in that hole, trying to handcuff him. His wrist was too small. He kept slipping through. He just couldn't hold him. The boy died calling for his mother three hundred feet away. So close. All that love, all those people. Nothing. Just a shaft into the earth big enough for a boy to fall into and a wrist too small to hold on to.

"Sergeant DeVito, this is Supervisor Ramsey. It's been quite a while since we had any action on the Saunders' tap. I'm sure everything's in order, but we have no current paperwork on that tap. I hope you understand. We haven't had official verification from your captain of your reassignment to this case, and we can't reveal this information to anyone but the officer assigned."

"Ma'am, I appreciate your conscientiousness and it'll not go unreported. But this is an emergency. We need that address now. A child's life is at stake. I'll take the responsibility on this myself. If you look at your old papers there, I was on this case from the very beginning. You don't want to cause a delay here that could be tragic. I'll take responsibility, I assure you."

Silence. Herb wished he was clairvoyant: what's the screw to turn to get you to do what I want? I'll do it. I'd do anything to get my babies back. Anything.

"All right. The number is 555-3329."

"Thank you."

He knew he had to move fast. If they called the station to confirm all this, DeVito would know. He'd be there in no time. He wasn't about to let them handle this. If you want something done right, do it yourself. No one else cares as much. They're my babies. My kids. I'll get them back. He swore it. He remembered the first time. The description of the car and the girls was everywhere. Porterfield let them go right through. He thought they were sleeping. He hadn't read his reports yet. He was going to at the Little Tavern. Not again Saunders swore. *They are my kids. Mine. I'll get them back. Nothing will stop me. I swear it! Tina. Molly. Do you hear me? I'm coming. Daddy's coming!'*

Chapter **2**

I WAS WATCHING MY FAVORITE WORKOUT SHOW. NOT DOING IT, mind you—just watching. Some lissome lass from L.A. was telling me "Three more, two more, one more, now switch to the other hand." I checked my lap. Best exercise program I'd ever seen. Gets my heart rate up to one hundred twenty for twenty minutes just sitting still. I'd run my two miles and done the stadium steps over at Falls Church High just to warm up for this. The phone rang.

"Hello. Leo Haggerty."

"Mr. Haggerty, are you the Leo Haggerty that's a private detective?" A woman's voice.

"I was the last time I checked. What can I do for you?"

"Well, I have a problem. Before I go into it, I'd like to ask you some questions, okay?"

"Sure. Let me just get a cup of coffee. Be right back." I went over and poured myself a cup. What the hell. I'd been interviewed by prospective clients before, so this was nothing new. Her voice was interesting: polite, restrained, controlled, and controlling. I felt like a big dog being calmed.

"Okay. What would you like to know?"

"As a detective, do you have a specialty, Mr. Haggerty?"

"Mostly I do missing persons work. Kidnappings, child snatching by parents, missing heirs, witness location, what have you. I do some background investigations, but not much. I'm bonded so I do some courier service work and some bodyguarding. That about covers it."

"Are you any good, Mr. Haggerty?"

"Well, since you put it that way, Ms. — I didn't get your name."

"I didn't give it and unless I decide to retain you, I won't."

"Okay. Am I any good? Good question. Yes, I am good. I'm very good. Sometimes that still isn't enough and I'd like to be better yet. Was I recommended to you, or did you get my name out of the phone book?"

"You were recommended to me, and very highly. Your reference said you would answer that question just about the way you did."

"It's nice to be predictable."

"That, I've been told, you are not. Why are you good, Mr. Haggerty?"

"Why am I good? I don't know. I have a face like a microphone. Everybody wants to talk into it." I continued to tick off my lustrous virtues. "I'm persistent as hell. Not out of duty, mind you. I'm just that way; loose ends drive me crazy. I check everything out. Twice. Then once again. Also I've got a pretty good imagination. Comes from a childhood as a chronic liar. I can explain anything. At one time or another I've probably tried to. Nothing's too bizarre to try out as an explanation. Basically, I turn up things other people miss and imagine possibilities other people don't. Sometimes that's all it takes. But then I never found Amelia Earhart either."

"Do you have any children, Mr. Haggerty?"

This was a line of questioning I'd never heard before.

"No."

"Are you married?"

"No."

"Have you ever been?"

"No."

"Ever been in love?"

"Too often."

"Please be serious. I assure you I am."

"Yes. I wasn't very good at it so I retired from the game. Rather, semiretired."

"What are your fees, Mr. Haggerty?"

"Three hundred and fifty dollars a day plus all expenses."

"Do you ever take a case for reasons other than money?"

I hate this kind of phone call. Every try to pay the rent with quince jelly?

"I try not to, especially when my bills are due. But if I can pay my bills I try to be imaginative about my fees. I've been known to barter services, for instance. The first thing is, what do you want me to do for you, and how long is it likely to take?"

She took a moment to decide if I was what she needed.

"Do you know the names Herbert and Margaret Saunders? Tina and Molly Saunders?"

Oh shit. "Yes I do. What can I do for you?"

"I'm Margaret Saunders. My husband has disappeared. I want you to find him for me. Please. Can you come out to the house today? Perhaps now?"

"Give me about an hour. It's Bethesda, isn't it?"

"Yes, let me give you directions."

"That won't be necessary. I grew up not too far from your house. I'll see you in about an hour, Mrs. Saunders."

Chapter 3

I SHOWERED AND DRESSED. SIGOURNEY WEAVER WAS ON A TALK show. I lingered at the knob before I turned it off. I've asked for her in my Christmas stocking for four years now. The closest I ever got was a tape of *Alien* from a girl who was sick of watching me moon over her.

I backed the Camaro out of the driveway and headed around the Beltway to Bethesda. The Homeland. I'm a rare bird in this town: a native, born and raised. Let me tell you this is one strange town. Like a snake, Washington sheds itself every four years. Everybody in goverment, which is the biggest game in town, is just passing through. They can run the country, but not the city they're staying in. To them, D.C. is just a giant motel, not a home. They make a mess of things and then move on. The maid'll be in to clean up.

I crossed the Cabin John Bridge into Maryland, got off at the River Road exit, and took a left onto Windbreak Lane. A leggy redhead jogged by plugged into her Sony Walkman. I hate those things. The middle class ghetto blasters. In Anacostia it's "it's in yo' ear motha fucker." In Bethesda its "What did you say? I can't hear you." It's just as narcissistic, only better behaved. The cold shoulder is connected to the flying finger.

I rolled slowly down the quiet tree-lined road. Welcome home. The Golden Ghetto. The promised land. I grew up here. These days I spend a lot of my time here or in Potomac or McLean. They can afford me. It won't be long before I'll be looking for the children of my classmates. The ones who made it back. Inflation rose faster than our aspirations or achievements, and few of us will live in the style we were accustomed to. I guess the kids I'll be looking for will be a lot like I was. There's a sinister dream here on these well-tended lanes: the dream of a place in time and space where you've "got it made" and you're "happy ever after;" that there's a formula of designer labels, prep schools and country clubs, acreage and address that will immunize you from pain and loss.

To some kids that elixir's still castor oil because this isn't their dream. This is the springboard for them. The given from which they'll fashion their own dreams. Their parents can't understand wanting something other than what they've struggled their whole lives for. So the kids turn the dream on its ear. They know what they don't want and little else. So they get drunk on the Chivas, smash up the Mercedes, steal from Bloomingdale's, flunk out of Landon, and hang themselves with alarming frequency.

I did all but the last. That's why I don't live here. It took my father ten years to get over the disappointment, but he did. Better late than never.

The house was typical Bethesda. A quarter acre for a quarter of a million dollars. Mature, well-tended trees. This was an older neighborhood. Maybe from the early sixties when the Beltway was built. With that concrete circle around the city allowing easy access anywhere, people spilled out as if the city had been unzipped. Thus was suburbia born.

I sat in the car thinking about the Saunders case. It was one of the most famous ones in Washington history. The biggest manhunt in years. Complete with grand foul-ups. What was the cop's name? Porterfield. He let them right through his fingers. Saunders tried to kill him one night in a bar. Damn near beat him to death. What a mess. Twin girls. How old were they? Seven? Eight? They'd gone down the street to go swimming at a neighbor's pool. Never seen again. I remembered the poster. Everywhere. The television pleas. I couldn't watch them. Well here we are. Time to go in.

I closed the door and looked up at the house. All the windows covered, no eyes outward. A house turned in on itself. I didn't want to go in. I felt like I do when I have to use a roadside rest room. You know it's going to be bad; it's just a question of how bad.

The door bell was a jangling electric buzz. After a long count it opened. A petite woman stood there. Her presence seemed as precarious as that of a leaf in a storm: holding on tenaciously in the wind, but just barely. I wondered if it was the translucence of her skin, the fineness of her hair that did it. She looked as if she might just wink out in an instant. Her body was stiff. Composed. Composure dearly bought. Just like her speaking voice on the phone.

"Mrs. Saunders. I'm Leo Haggerty. May I come in?"

"Please. I'm sorry. I thought for a second it was Herb coming back. But he wouldn't ring the door bell, would he?"

She waved me in. The house was almost unfurnished. What there was was strictly functional and not very expensive.

She saw my eyes move around the room and began an oft-repeated and unnecessary explanation, "After Herb lost his job, we really couldn't afford to live here. For a little while we made do by selling a lot of our belongings. Then even that wouldn't do it. Now we're here by the bank's graces. We pay what we can. We can stay here until the girls return. That's what they said. We told them we couldn't leave. What if they come back and we're not here? They're only twelve, just children you know."

A lifetime vigil. A lighthouse on the river Styx waiting for a boat, a cloaked ferryman, and the first ever return trip from the far shore.

I sat myself down on the sofa and faced Mrs. Saunders.

She stood there and asked me, "Would you care for something to drink or eat?"

I requested a cup of coffee just to have something for my hands to hold. A ceramic shield from the awful stillness of the place.

She returned with coffee, creamer, sugar, a spoon, and some cookies on a plate. I prepared my coffee and leaned back on the sofa. "How long has your husband been missing, Mrs. Saunders?"

"Just overnight. He wasn't here when I came home from work. That was unusual. He hasn't been outside the house for days. I thought he'd gone for a walk or a drive. He does that sometimes. Used to be he'd ride for hours. Now he's only gone a little while. So I expected him home. Well, when he wasn't home for dinner, I called some places he'd gone to in the past. Nobody'd seen him. Well, it got later and later. I couldn't sleep. I just sat up looking out the window for him. I was sure every car I heard would be his. But they weren't. I began to get frightened."

She looked away from me.

"It was just like before all over again. I just couldn't take it."

She clasped her hand over her mouth and bit into herself. It didn't help. The tears just rolled down her cheeks.

"Oh God, oh God. Please find him for me. He's all I've got left. I just can't go on alone. Please."

"I'll try. I'll give it my best shot. I really will."

They were weak words I hurled into that hurricane of sorrow. Like going to throw the javelin and finding only a toothpick in your hand.

She turned away.

Please excuse me. I'll be right back."

She got up and walked swiftly from the room, her hand again in her mouth.

I took a deep breath. Why wasn't I a florist? Something

optimistic, upbeat. Hell, florists sell funeral wreaths too. There's no escaping it. I stood up and walked around. The dining room was dark and empty. The only thing missing was a large spider spinning a web with everyone entangled in it, waiting silently until it was complete. I heard the sink drain from upstairs and Mrs. Saunders' returning steps.

I returned to my seat. She looked at a piece of paper in her hands. It was hard to pretend that I hadn't seen her distress. I decided to stop trying.

"I'm sorry, Mrs. Saunders. This must be a hellish reminder."

"Reminder? Everything's a reminder. Every child I see, every parent. Everyone who is anywhere, present and accounted for, is a reminder."

She looked around the almost empty rooms.

"You know, we had everything. We had it all." She shook her head. "We had nothing. It was all on loan."

The foreclosure must have been hell.

"The girls. Christina and Molly? Isn't that right?"

"Yes."

"Do you have any other children?"

"No." She looked down at the paper again. "We talked about it. Herb wanted to. To start over. Recreate a family. I wasn't too old. We tried. I guess deep down I couldn't go through it again—loving them and losing them. I never could get pregnant again. After a while we stopped trying. It's too late now." She looked down at the paper again. "That's why you've got to find Herb for me. He's all I've got left. I couldn't make it for a minute on my own. I only made it because I had him to take care of." She nervously fingered the paper.

"May I see that?"

"Oh, yes. I think Herb must have written it yesterday before he left. He hasn't sounded like that in quite a while. It was upstairs on my pillow."

It was a letter. No envelope. The postmark would have been the far side of hell.

> Dear Maggie, Dearest Maggie:
> The Devil spoke today. He did. I swear it. He tried to dance on me and he slipped and fell. He think's he's so smart. Well, he fell far from grace once, and he's done it again, and I have him. This time I do. I know it. We're brothers and he doesn't know it. He's so proud, so proud. I'm going to get the girls back. I swear it. I promise you, Maggie girl, it will be all over. We'll sleep at night and have our dreams in the day. Please hold on. Please wait for me. I'm sorry to do this to you. I know I haven't been much of a husband or a comfort to you. I just want you to know I could never have made it this long without you and I love you beyond words. I'm ready. All this time I've made myself ready. I am pure, I am white hot. I am hard. I will not fail. I will return with the girls. I promise you. We'll be young again.
> Love, Herb.

"You said he hasn't sounded like this in a while?"

"Yes. Right after the girls disappeared, Herb really fell apart. He was depressed, paranoid. He drank a lot. Made a lot of accusations. To our friends, to the police. When he drank, he would talk like that. But it hasn't happened in a long time. I checked to see if he had bought any liquor. We don't keep any in the house, and I couldn't find any bottles. Frankly, he hadn't been out of the house for, oh, three or four days so I would have been surprised if he had gone out."

"Was that typical for him?"

Typical. I don't know what's typical anymore. Herb went through fairly discrete stages. He'd seem to get an idea fixed in his mind and hold on to it, and then just as suddenly he'd give it up. Act normal for a few days or weeks and then get another idea that would dominate him. He'd become obsessed by it. That hasn't happened in a while. Recently he's just settled into a quiet watchfulness. No grand ideas, no tension."

She shook her head. "This just took the heart out of him. Herb was just ruined. That's how he lost his job. He just couldn't work. He couldn't think about anything but the girls. Mind you, I don't blame him for anything. I'm just thankful he hasn't killed himself. His habits changed. He stopped sleeping. He was sure he'd miss a phone call or a knock at the door. He didn't eat and lost a lot of weight. He's had a lot of phases. This sitting around the house seemed a lot like his waiting stage.

"He used to dig up people's lawns, go barging into houses. You could never tell what he'd think was a clue. Then he gave up on clues. That's why this outburst surprises me. Why now? And I'm worried about him. I've often thought that I'd lose Herb to insanity as surely as I've lost my children, and I'm afraid that's what this letter is. Please bring him back. He thinks I've helped him make it. If I didn't have him to love and care about I'd have had nothing and I'd have killed myself. Bring him back to me. Please. He's all I have left."

"I'll try. May I have this letter?"

She stood up and went to a small secretary in the corner. "I went out and had a copy made this morning for you. I'd prefer to hold the original. I also have a picture for you. It's not very recent."

I took it from her hand. "How different does he look?"

"Well, he's still clean shaven, but now, he keeps his head shaved too." She looked back at the picture. "Other than that his cheeks are more hollowed out, but that's pretty much what he looks like."

"You said you'd called his friends to see if he was there?"

"No, not his friends. Herb has no friends anymore. Rather,

I called the old bars he used to go to when he sounded like that letter and the police station. Nobody has seen him."

"What kind of a car does he drive?"

"It's a 1977 Dodge Aspen station wagon."

"License number?"

"Uh, BHA 313."

I'd ask about credit card numbers if the trail got cold. "Did he pack anything?"

"No, nothing."

"That fit with his promise that he'd be back soon. Okay, who else knows him very well or was involved in the case that might help me understand him better? He may really be lost in a landscape of his own. If I can map that at all it'll help me find him."

"Well, there's his old therapist, Dr. Prentice, and of course, Sergeant Peter DeVito. He's been in charge of the investigation from the beginning. He may know Herb best of all."

I wrote down the names and addresses. I tried to find a soft side to my next question, but there weren't any. "Mrs. Saunders, some of your husband's behavior is a little unusual. Does he have any other, uh, eccentricities?"

She thought for a second and then said, "Yes, let me check. Please come on down to the basement."

I followed her down the stairs to a large basement, largely empty except for the far corner. We went over to it, and she pulled on the overhead lamp. There was a map full of red pins, and stacks of notebooks. Mrs. Saunders was rummaging in a pile of boxes along the wall. Looking up she said, "Herb kept his own maps and notes of each lead in the search." I looked over at the boxes. They were full of books on survival skills, martial arts, wilderness crafts, and detective and military operations manuals. She stood up and looked at me, hands on her hips, "It's gone."

"What is?"

"The bag. The black bag. It's gone."

"What black bag?"

"Herb had a black bag he carried with him everywhere for a while. He even handcuffed it to himself."

"What was in it?"

"I don't know. It was always locked. I'll tell you the truth, I didn't want to know. In those days Herb was very close to getting committed. He'd gotten into some fights and damaged some property, like I said. Anyway, I didn't want to know. I just wanted it to go away. He calmed down and put the bag away. It's been, oh, three years now." She stood looking imploringly at the boxes hoping to coax the bag home by the sheer intensity of her will. I took her by the elbow and turned out the light. In the darkness I slowly guided her to the stairs and up. When we came back to the sitting room I helped her to a chair.

"I'll let myself out, Mrs. Saunders. I'll keep you informed of anything I learn." I reached into my coat and gave her my card. "Call if you want to. Anytime. I'll return the calls as soon as I can." I turned to go.

"Mr. Haggerty, what about your fee?" Her chin was up.

I thought about it. I had some money in the bank. My bills would get paid this month. This guy could be so lost in himself as to be unfindable, or he could be sitting on the stoop. I could look for him for a while without feeling the pinch or needing to split time with another case. "Tell you what. I gave you a lot of stuff about how good I am. That's why you asked me out here, right? Give me a chance to prove it. If I don't find him by the end of the week, then there's no charge. Maybe I'm just not as good as I'm cracked up to be. If I find him, then we'll talk about a fee."

I didn't give her a chance to argue. I wasn't about to dicker nickels and dimes with this lady and so I went deaf and blind on my way out. At my car I turned back. I thought of the woman trapped inside. A scream looking for a voice.

Chapter 4

JUDGEMENT DAY. JUDGEMENT DAY. OUR FATHER WHO ART HERE on the doorstep is gonna cut your heart out Satan and release all those from your domination. Open up.

Chanting that mantra to himself, Herb Saunders hopped from foot to foot, a hyperactive flamingo. The black bag jingled as it hung from his wrist. Using the reverse directory in the public library to get the address, he wondered what the hell a guy from Rockville had been doing in his neighborhood. He'd soon find out. He'd rung the bell twice. No answer. He hoped Maggie wasn't too upset. It would be over soon. He thanked God the mailman came early. After he'd gone he rifled it and gotten enough: a name and a pretext. Mr. Justin Randolph, hi-tech computer whiz. We'll plug you into my bag, Herr Randolph, and see how many functions you've got. He unlocked the bag, slipped his hand in, and closed it around his greeting. The door locks turned. Saunders was vertiginous, pulled through the portal by his own frenzy.

The door was opened by a woman in a uniform. Saunders leaned forward. For a moment she shrank back ever so slightly. "May I help you, sir?"

Saunders closed the bag and smiled. "Uh, yes. Of course. Mr. Randolph please. I'm Mr. Herbert, Sanford Herbert, from the computer company. We were going to discuss the new terminals he wanted installed."

"Oh, there must be some mistake, sir. Mr. Randolph left today for a week."

"Was he alone?"

"Pardon me?"

"I mean, was he travelling with anyone? Our Miss Parsons was supposed to meet us here. I wondered if they left together. She may have gone with him. Perhaps it was to be a working week."

"No. He left by himself."

"I see. Could you give me the address or phone number where he was going? I really must contact him. The deal on this hardware must be completed right away or there'll be a 10% escalator added. He'd be hopping mad if that happened." He smiled at her sending her a telepathic message: We wouldn't want that now, would we little Miss Starch 'n Glow.

"I'm sorry. I just come in and clean once a week. I stay over when he's out of town. All I know is that Mr. Randolph has a house in North Carolina. He goes there for vacations."

"Do you have a phone number there?"

"No. There's no phone there. He says he likes the privacy. Calls it his retreat." She smiled at him like a doting auntie explaining her favorite nephew's latest prank.

"I see. Well where in North Carolina is it? I really need to be in touch with him."

"Let me think. I usually don't pay attention to these things. You know — come in, do my job, and leave."

"Has he ever mentioned anything about the place, you know, anything unusual, memorable, that sticks in your mind?"

She squinted in thought. "Well, his place is at the beach. There's always sand around when he comes back. It's in everything. I think the town's name is Beach something or something Beach."

"Yes, yes. Go on." Come on, think dammit.

"I remember something he said. There is a ferry there. Goes out to some island. He was late returning one time and said the ferry had been delayed and he was stuck on the island for hours. That's all really. I usually don't see Mr. Randolph to talk with. I just do my work and leave."

"Listen. Thank you. You've been very helpful, really. I'll try to track him down from what you've said." Saunders gave her his best conspiratorial smile. "This deal means a lot to me. Commission on sales, you know. Tell me, how long has Mr. Randolph had his beach house, do you know? I might try to interest him in some terminals for there if the wiring isn't too old. I know he likes to stay on top of things." C'mon, just one prole helping another.

"Well, let's see. I've been cleaning for him for ten years now. Is it ten? Harry died in October of '73. So, yes, it's ten years, almost eleven. He bought the place, I'd been here, oh three years, I guess. That'd make it 1977. That's about right. Yeah, 1977. My grandson, Tommy, was born then and I asked to take off a week to go see my daughter. He said it was okay. He was going down to settle on the place and wanted to give it a last look-see so he didn't need me here to clean."

"Well, again, thank you. You've been very helpful. Have a nice day." They exchanged smiles, and she slowly pushed the door closed. Saunders started back to his car, stopped, and looked up at the house. Small decals warned that the house was wired with an alarm system. So much for the idea of returning at night to ransack the place and get an address. Too risky. He needed to get on his way.

Sitting in his car he began to plot. He too wanted to disappear. No trails. He'd need a new car, a rental one, and cash to pay for things. Leave this car in a lot at National, then get a rental nearby. First the bank for some cash. He needed to move fast. DeVito'd be on to him any time now. Opening the glove compartment he took out a map of the southeastern U.S. After folding it over to the North Carolina coast line he began circling towns with the word beach and

looking for the black dotted line indicating a ferry. He worked
up from the South Carolina border. There it was. Bogue
Beach and the Pamlico Ferry. Gotcha! He could barely sit
still. He was in a frenzy of anticipation and euphoric with
hatred. He started the car with a vow: Mr. Justin Randolph,
when we meet you'll wish you'd croaked with your first cry.
I swear it.

Chapter 5

I WALKED BACK TO THE CAR AND GOT IN. FIRST STOP: DR. Prentice. I pulled away and headed for his address on Wisconsin Avenue. It was a converted home on the edge of Chevy Chase, not the comedian. The brass plate said Randall Williams, Ph.D. and Charles Prentice, Ph.D., P.C. I went inside. The secretary looked up and said, "May I help you?"

"I hope so. I'm here to see Dr. Prentice. It's rather important. It's about a patient of his."

"Oh, I'm sorry. Dr. Prentice is out of town. He's giving an address at a convention in Tampa."

"Is his partner, Dr. Williams, available?"

"Let me see."

She buzzed him from the switchboard. The intercom crackled, "Yes, Sydney?"

"Dr. Williams, there's a man here to see Dr. Prentice. He said it's very important, about a patient of his." She looked up at me earnestly.

"I'll be right up. Thank you."

Dr. Randall Williams was short and solidly built. His pointed beard mirrored the arch of his eyebrows. His smile was warm, and there was a touch of elf in the man.

"Randall Williams." We shook hands.

"Leo Haggerty." I fished out my license. "I'm a private investigator looking for Mr. Herbert Saunders. I understand he was a patient of Dr. Prentice's. I wanted to talk with him about Mr. Saunders' emotional state. To help me locate him."

"I'm sorry, Mr. Haggerty. I don't know the case well enough to give you any useful information. However, even if I did I would not be at liberty to reveal that to you. Professional ethics forbid it. A recent court decision here in Maryland made it clear that even if you told me Mr. Saunders was an imminent danger to himself or anyone else, neither I nor Dr. Prentice could reveal anything about him. Without his consent, of course. And if you had that you'd have found him and not need our help anyway. I'm sorry I can't be of any further help. Now if you'll excuse me I have a patient coming in and I need to do some preparing. Good day."

We shook hands and I shrugged. I'd seen a lot of dead ends in my day. Most weren't as polite as this. The information would have been helpful, but not crucial. Mrs. Saunders said that the police sergeant Peter DeVito probably knew her husband best.

The police station wasn't too far so I figured I'd head straight up there. If DeVito was in, maybe he and I could talk over lunch. Maybe we couldn't talk at all. I never know with cops how they'll react to me. Lots of them see me as a nuisance, an intrusion, a troublemaker. Sometimes I am. Hopefully they deserve the trouble I'm making. Some of them know their limitations: budgets that you can't budge, caseloads that become overloads, docket backups, and unspeedy trials. Sometimes they welcome what I can do that they can't and they're helpful. Cops like that aren't the rule in my experience. They are a pleasant surprise. I hoped Sergeant Peter DeVito would be one.

I jogged up the station house steps, let a lady cop through the door, and went inside. The cop on desk duty asked me what I wanted. I showed him my license and said I wanted Sergeant DeVito. If his face was any indicator, he was passing a kidney stone. I told him it was about the Saunders case. He made a quick recovery and got on the intercom.

"Hey Pete, there's a P.I. here about the Saunders case."

"On my way down."

Pete DeVito slogged grimly down the stairs fighting the tide of his own reluctance. He was in his fifties with a steel gray flattop, a rebuilt nose, and no laugh lines at all. His gait had the awkward roll of a weight lifter. He had the size too. We shook hands.

"Pete DeVito."

"Leo Haggerty."

"Unless you've got two kids to turn in out in your car, I'm not sure we've got anything to talk about."

"I wish I did. But it's about Herb Saunders. He's disappeared. Left a crazy note for his wife. She says he hasn't been like this in years. She also says you know him as well as anyone. I was hoping you'd give me some clues as to where to look for him."

DeVito shrugged and looked at the clock, "All right. Hey Nick. I'm goin' to lunch with this guy. Be back in an hour. Okay?"

"Yeah, Sarge."

DeVito went back up and came down with his jacket on. His holster now discreetly covered, he could walk among the civilians. We went out, and DeVito looked up and down Wisconsin Avenue trying to pick up the scent of food in the air and decide where to eat.

"There's a Chinese place down the road. They've got a back room. We can talk."

We went to his car and down to the restaurant. The place was packed. DeVito slid around the line and went to the hostess. A little head nodding and badge showing and the owner appeared. More head nodding, a little arm waving, a lot of smiling all around. DeVito waved me up front. We went around the corner to a cordoned off banquet room, marked This Section Closed. The sign was turned around and we were seated.

DeVito leaned back in his chair and took the menus from the waitress. I looked at it and ordered, as did he. She slipped silently away.

"All right. Herb Saunders has disappeared. As of when?"

"Yesterday."

"You said he wrote a letter to Maggie?"

"Yeah. Here it is."

He looked at it and handed it back to me. "Vintage Herb. He ain't been like that for years. Not since he used to get the crackpot calls and letters. He'd get so psyched up over a 'lead' he'd be wired, wouldn't sleep. He'd pace up and down. Show up at the station all hours. Then he'd crash. Drink himself blind to come down. That's when he'd be trouble.

"How so?"

"Oh, he'd get in fights. He'd decide to search a place. Like at 3 A.M. with a crowbar for a key. Sometimes I thought he had a death wish. Just looking for someone to put his lights out. Problem was he's a tough cookie, and with a little sour mash propellant in him he was hard to bring down. I went out and brought him in a few times. Sat up all night with him, talking, pouring coffee into him. Getting him through the night into the next day."

"How long have you been on this case?"

"Since day one. I took some time off for a while. Thought maybe a fresh perspective would turn something up. It didn't. So I asked to be put back on it. Not too long ago, actually." The waitress returned with our food. DeVito dug right in and after a couple of wolfish swallows, stopped and wiped his mouth.

"Listen, when you came in talking about the Saunders case I got short not 'cause I don't care. Believe me I care, but I've got no patience left. Too many kooka-rookas have tried to get their kicks on this case and I'm getting too old to still be nice about it. You can help, great; you're a wacko then piss off. Mind you, I follow up everything. Everything. I just ain't polite any more."

"You have any theories about it?"

"Theories, yeah. You got only a couple of ways to go on a case like this." He counted on his fingers, "Runaway, murder, or abduction. Never been a shred of evidence of a runaway situation. No reason to suspect a simple homicide. Why? What reason? Who would want to simply kill them? The family was solid, no underworld connections, no drugs, no gambling. No need to teach them a lesson. That leaves abduction. Why? Money? No ransom was ever demanded, no political extortion. They weren't a prominent family. No, that just leaves us with the perverts. My theory is somebody stole those kids to abuse them and then killed them when he was done, and they've been dead a long time."

"Sometimes they don't. They show up years later."

"Yeah, yeah, I know. Usually that's real little kids stolen by crazy women who want babies. So they take care of the kid and don't hurt it. Problem is we've never had a woman associated with this case. Porterfield saw a man in that car."

"What about that California case. The kidnapper was a man?"

"Yeah, but this is different."

"How so?"

DeVito put his face in his palm and looked away and then back at me. Hard. "Okay, I don't know why but I'll show you something when we get back to the station. The only lead we ever had."

"Okay. Thanks."

"Maybe you can do something with this. Find a new angle. Lord knows I don't know any more about this case than I did the day it happened." The exhaustion of four years of keeping the sails of hope up in the dead calm of this mystery showed on DeVito's face. He shook his head, "It's a killer you know."

I nodded.

"You know what a 'cannibal case' is?"

"Yeah."

"Well this is one of them. It eats up everyone it touches. Me, Porterfield, the Saunders, all the families, my men. I had to take a leave of absence after about a year on the case. My wife was ready to leave me. I had a burn in my gut. You'd a thought I was gargling with Drano. I had a hotline rigged into the house. I was up and out all the time, any day of the week for a year following leads. I wanted to find those kids so bad. Just give'em back to their folks and make all that hurt go away. Jesus, we never made one bit of progress on this. Son of a bitch was a genius or just lucky. I always thought it was a drifter. Somebody just passing through. A one-man plague stalking this country. 'The kid killer.' Someday we'll arrest some 60-year-old vagrant, and in the drunk tank he'll start to talk and it'll all unravel. It'll dwarf anything we ever imagined."

DeVito ate some more and began to talk again. He'd probably never been asked how he felt about the case, the helpless helper, and he had a lot to empty himself of. I sipped some tea.

"That's what this case did to me. Made me believe in magic. You know early on I did community work. Lots of 'safety tips.' Do this and you'll be okay. Don't do this, it's dangerous. Shit. Brave talk. The only ones safe are the dead! Really tossed me over. I got paranoid. I'd look at my kids. They were older, but just as vulnerable. Nothing I could do. Couldn't save them from this thing out there. I couldn't find these kids. Man, I really knew where Saunders was coming from."

"You ever suspect him?"

"Oh hell, yes. Early on. Had to. Case like this odds are it's not a parent, but that don't make it impossible. Oh, we kept him under surveillance for quite a while. Lie detector. The whole shebang. That's how I got called to pick him up from the bars. No, he was clean all the way. Really killed me to have done that after a while. The guy really loved his kids you know. He'd never have touched them. That I know. That's a fact that's true. Maybe the only thing I know about this case. But I do know that Herb Saunders lived for those kids. Now he's dying for them. I think about the helplessness. You love them so much. They're so much a part of you. I think that's what love is. You let someone get as important to you as yourself. You hurt their hurt. You know those kids are in pain and frightened as long as they're away from you. Every moment you know that pain is there. Until it's over one way or another you know it's pain they feel and you feel it. You want to stop it. You'd do anything to stop it. And you sit there, helpless to end the pain. It'll make you crazy. Herb couldn't stand that. I think the drinking, the fights were ways to stop the pain, the helplessness."

"You ever suspect Porterfield?"

DeVito chuckled sadly. "Oh yeah. I suspect everyone. Put a tail on myself for a while. You know, a schizo, a split personality. Had to ask myself why I was so obsessed by this case. It's my nightmare. It's everybody's nightmare. Somebody just tears a hunk out of you and you can't give it up for dead. What if they come back someday? The guilt would kill you. What if. Those two words'll make you crazy. What if. What if. You step right through a doorway and what is, is gone. There's no time. Limbo, man. I'd rather go to hell. It's the waiting that does you in. You can't go on. You can't go back. You're frozen there. Your guts being torn out forever."

I thought of the eagles eating at Prometheus. It took Hercules to rescue him. Half man, half god. It would take more than me or DeVito had to put an end to this.

"I think that's what happened to Herb. He 'what iffed' himself right around the bend. Seems like it's a one way street to me and Herb didn't know how to go in reverse. He never did."

I tried to redirect DeVito. "What about Porterfield?"

"Oh yeah. Sorry. I get lost in this sometimes. Porterfield. Yeah, we checked him out. A cop gets a kid's trust pretty easily. Good access there. He gave us our only lead. Could have been a throwaway, a fake to misdirect us. It never panned out. Maybe there was no man. But we found the car. Maybe Porterfield planted it. We watched him for a long time. He never did anything suspicious. His fuck-up cost him his career. Probably more. He was disciplined by a review board. They didn't need to. The man would have killed himself if he thought it would get the kids back. Wanted to be transferred to the investigating team. Rode around the clock for days looking for the car. Just like all of us, it ate him up. He took an early retirement. He was a good man who made a mistake. Everything else about him got lost or forgotten. He was the man who let them slip through his fingers and that's it. One hell of an epitaph, I'll tell you. People may forgive you, but life's a pretty ruthless proposition." DeVito wiped his mouth and signaled for the check. We split it and left a healthy tip — perhaps some kind of offering to a god of mercy indeterminate. DeVito looked at me with baffled sadness. A fisherman who'd tried to throw a net over tomorrow and came up empty. We left together.

Chapter 6

AT THE STATION DEVITO WENT BACK TO THE RECORDS ROOM. He came back with a sealed parcel. "Let's go down to the viewing room. It's in the basement."

I trotted after him.

DeVito opened the pouch and took out a video cassette. He turned on a TV monitor and made some adjustments to the attached recorder. He looked back at me. "This is the only lead we've ever had on this case. We found the car Porterfield saw two days later. We went over that thing like it was a flying saucer. Nothing. I mean nothing. . . . But this tape. Had to have been left there on purpose. This bastard was too careful. It was either a message to us or so unrelated that he didn't care. I tend to believe the latter because we never got anywhere with this. We talked to every tape maker, distributor, sales outlet in the whole metropolitan area. I talked to an expert on the West Coast. The only thing we know is it's local and amateur. We looked up the people in this in every mug book in the area. I was on 14th Street for days talking to everybody down there. Christ, I even got picked up in a sweep. Nothing."

DeVito turned off the lights, came back, and sat next to me. "Hold on to your seat. I'm going to show you an act that's got so many Xs, nobody's old enough to see it." He aimed the remote control at the set like a sword, and it lit up.

There was a man standing in the center of the screen. He had a black hood over his face and nothing else on. In his left hand was a leash. At the end of it on all fours was a nude woman with very close-cropped blond hair. She looked straight into the camera with a face that looked older than time. The man jerked on the leash and barked, "come." He began to walk across the barren room with the woman crawling on all fours. The leash snapped again. "Sit." The woman gasped and dropped her ass to the ground. The man undid the choke collar and strode away from her. He turned crisply and clapped his hands. "Come." The woman moved quickly across the floor to him, her ass wagging from side to side. My lunch was starting to clot. The trainer snarled, "down." She dropped on her elbows and knees and slowly rolled her head and eyes up at him. "Roll over, bitch." She rolled over and assumed the canine submissive position: hind legs apart, forelegs folded up, throat bared. He knelt next to her and stroked and probed her everywhere, cooing "good girl, good girl." He stood again and went off screen and returned with a chair. He sat and commanded, "up." The woman got on her knees and worked her way between his legs. He stroked her under the chin and behind the ears. He said, "suck" and she did. Her machine mouth drove on as relentless as progress. I'd had enough. DeVito turned it off, hit the lights, looked at me, and shook his head. "You see why I'm not optimistic? That's one hateful bastard if that's him." He put the cassette back in its pouch and sealed it again. I wished the images would recede as quickly as that. We shook hands, and he wished me good luck. I told him I'd keep him posted. We trudged up from the basement. On the way to my car I knew what I had to do. The thought left me more than a little cold. Time to talk to Lester Kroll, king of the trolls.

Chapter 7

FATHER AUGUSTUS SHANNON THOUGHT, *ONE MORE TO GO, then I can relax. Not the best attitude I know, but my back has been killing me. Maybe I need orthopedic shoes. Maybe one leg's longer than the other. Who knows. Just get me through this day.* He took off his wire-rimmed glasses and rubbed his eyes. He squinted when he put them back on and waited to hear the door close on the other side. The penitent began, "Bless me, Father, for I have sinned. My last confession was . . . too long ago, Father." Father Shannon remembered that the last person was a stranger, a face new to the flock. He'd been here long enough to know most of his parish by voice. The silence went on for a while. Father Augustus said, "Yes, my son?"

"That's a good point, Father. Am I your son? I mean, do you think there's a place in your heaven for me, Father? I've gone quite aways astray."

"God's love is infinite as is his forgiveness. Repent your ways and all things are possible." Father Shannon had often heard this defiance and doubt in his adolescent congregation members.

"That's an interesting concept. Let me tell you my story first. I've refined myself quite a bit over the years. It's nice to be able to sit here in the dark, though I wish it were cooler, and tell someone about myself. Unburden myself, as it were. I mean that's what confession is, isn't it? Oh, by the way, before we begin. What I say here is confidential, isn't it?

I mean absolutely confidential. You Catholics are ones for absolutes?"

"What you say here is absolutely confidential without exception, provided it is a confession of sin in hopes of reconciliation with your God." Father Shannon was used to the need for certainty among penitents that this was an inviolate secrecy. It was essential to the task of seeking God's forgiveness that they be free to pursue it without fear of the censure of their fellow men. "You said 'you Catholics.' Are you not a Catholic, my son?"

"Oh, I'm not sure what I am these days." The man laughed. "First off, it's been quite a while, as I said. Seven years to be precise. Frankly, I didn't recognize you." The man laughed again.

"You wouldn't. I was assigned to this parish after Father Simons retired last year."

"Well, that changes things a bit." There was a pause, then, "This will do though. Let me tell you a story about myself. It's quite illuminating, really opened up my eyes to reality. Taught me a lot of lessons about myself that I've been pursuing ever since. When I was a younger man I sought the company of prostitutes. Unusual ones, for I sought unusual pleasures. The details are unnecessary, but I was pursuing my pleasure with one, a woman I had used quite often. I was lost in myself enacting our favorite game as I always did, when she started to laugh. She had looked up at us in the mirror and was laughing at me. I suddenly realized she had been laughing at me all the time. I stopped playing with her and began to beat her. I smashed her face. That mocking mouth I emptied of teeth. I hauled her around by her hair, slamming her head into the wall. Pretty soon there was blood everywhere. I took her head in my hands and looked into her face. She looked like a slam-dunked jelly donut. And what do you suppose I learned in that moment, Father? Let me tell you. I saw that there was no one there to laugh at me. There was no place for her to hide. I had reeled her entire being up from the depths like one of those grotesque lantern fish, so poorly adapted to the surface that they just lay there stunned. So did she. All of her was on the surface. Those bulging eyes looking at me for mercy, for an end to it all. I had turned her inside out like a pocket and emptied her of everything, every wish, every dream, every secret. Her life was reduced to one simple sentence: Don't hurt me. That was all there was. A simple purity to our relationship. I could inflict pain or not. She would suffer or not. There was nothing else. There's nothing like pain to bring people together. I'd never felt closer to anyone in my whole life. I wanted to thank her for having let me learn that beautiful lesson from her. So I let her live. I fixed her first. I really don't know if she lived through that night or not. Capricious mercy pleased me also. I had found the key to grasping the mystery of other people. They're so slippery and elusive. Don't you find that, Father? It's so hard to get the true measure of a person, to know, really know, if their heart is pure. Father? Oh Father, please don't go mute on me. We've only just begun. You wouldn't want me to leave angry would you?"

"Oh, no. No. Don't go. I'm here. I'm listening. Please don't go. Go on with your story."

"If you insist, Father. You do wish it, do you not?"

"Yes, Yes. Please go on," he said reluctantly.

"Very good, Father. Well, over the years I refined myself. I came to know myself much better. Actually, being here is the inevitable extension of all my evolution to date, but more of that later. That dear girl had taught me how to heal that terrible separateness between me and other people, that mystery. With my new tools people were known to me, simple and clear, straightforward, no deception, no lies. Oh I hate liars. I had solved the mystery. I had my hands on truth. How many philosophers can make that claim, I ask you. When

I ask a question, I get answers. You'd best believe that." The stranger stopped abruptly.

Father Shannon moved closer to the screen. He couldn't tell if the stranger was still there. Hope and dread churned in him as he peered into the lattice work that separated them.

The stranger began anew. "I'm sure you're hoping to hear of a traumatic childhood, beatings, abuse, abandonment. No. Sorry. Not so. My parents aren't divorced, alcoholic, poor. They never beat me. Not once. In fact, they never denied me a thing. I hardly remember them at all. They had little impact on me or I on them."

"I remember as a child I used to destroy my toys. And my mama would tell me that was a 'no-no.' I hated being told no. I wanted to do whatever I wanted, no limits, no nos. I've always broken rules. My will, my way. Do what I want. Did my mama tell me no once too often or not enough? Who knows? Can you believe what a fragile species we are if I'm the result of a no too few? Maybe I'm a biochemical glitch? Does it matter? Let me tell you I've studied mankind for these last few years now, and I'm not that strange, you know. Everyone wants to do what I do at some time. What do you think the families I've destroyed would do to me if they found me? Pray for me? Not likely, Father, not likely. But I'm sure you will, won't you?" The stranger laughed. "Think about it, Father. I am wish unlimited, power without end, no bounds. Perhaps I'm not so strange after all. I'm part of all men, unbound. Am I not superior? Let me tell you, Father, I sleep like a baby. I am successful, respected, comfortable. Life is simple, clean. I don't know anxiety, sadness, guilt, shame, depression, insecurity, doubt. No painful emotions. I know joy, contentment, happiness."

"Are you not lonely, my son, for the company or the love of others?" Father Shannon barely got his words out.

"Lonely? No Father. Happiness is my self. Do I miss the love of others? I could just as soon ask you if you miss the love of a roasted chicken, for that's what you all are to me—food."

"What do you think, Father? Can you answer me? Is there a place in your heaven for me?"

"God loves all. All who would turn to his ways, no matter how late, how far they have strayed. You were gifted with an immortal soul in his image. You can lose it, but you can't destroy it."

Fingers snaked through the grate and clutched it. "Oh no, Father? Can't destroy it? Let me tell you I've made people turn on themselves like cannibals to escape me. There's nothing I can't make a person do. Give me three hours alone with you, Father, and you'd . . ." the stranger's breath came rapidly.

"I'm sorry, Father. I'm here to seek forgiveness for my sins. I'm sorry I lost control like that. It's been quite a long time. Very unseemly of me. Where was I? You've confused me. I'm going to have to go back to the beginning. There was a time you'd have rued those words, Father. But I'm beyond that now. I have worked hard to purge myself of anger. I never really was angry, you know. But there was this frenzy. I was like a child at Christmas with a new toy when I was opening a person up—when I was getting close. Had to control that. I lost my head a couple of times. Got overzealous and that was that. Lost them. Jesus, that used to infuriate me. I'd have to go out and get another one. Right away. That was dangerous, let me tell you. But I was young. I needed to learn discipline. It's a game of inches. Ha, ha. I like that. Well anyway, you know sometimes I'm not sure it's the pain I'm after. I mean it works. But I sometimes think it's breaking the taboos I crave.

"Nothing is forbidden. It just happens that 'don't hurt me' is such a big no-no. I hate masochists. That's why I left the club. You know I realized that the game was just that: a game. If I'd been just into the pain I could have stayed there. Lord, there were some people you could do anything to. But they wanted the pain so that lost its appeal to me. It was doing what other people didn't want done that I adored. That look in that girl's eyes showed me the way. I could never play the game anymore.

"The pain is just a tool, you see. Kind of like prayer is for you, I guess. I bet I get better results, Father. Does God answer all prayers, Father? My people answer all my calls. Have you ever seen the human soul, Father? Well I have. It's a goggle-eyed shrieking thing that shakes all over and wets itself. If that's God's image, good luck."

"God answers all prayers, son. The answer is not always yes."

"Oh that's good. I like that, Father. I do. Excellent. Well, let's see. No-nos, no-nos. There is no no I am subject to. No realm where you can evade me. No action, no thoughts, no feelings, but that which I and my tools will to be. I am in control, my will, my possession. There is no secret, no separation, no hiding, no mystery. The inside is outside. The pain focuses the totality of their being. My every movement yields a corresponding response. I am everything to that person. A god, if you wish. I learned this on the winos of this country. Perfecting my art, you see. Trimming the herd. Cutting out the weak, sick, those unfit to survive. No one lamented them. They died without leaving a trace in our society. They had removed themselves from their families and friends. No one missed them. As I grew older I reached greater heights of dexterity and discipline; I once kept one alive for thirty hours. Thirty hours. It defies belief. I did things medicine would say was impossible. I tried to research it. Apparently no records are kept. It's a lost art. Well, as I grew older the demands began to exhaust me. It requires almost constant effort. Any respite and the damn things crawl back under a rock. So I studied. This led me to my next great discovery. You know in some ways you're right, Father. The soul or spirit may or may not be indestructible, but it's a damn sight hardier than the tissue. I needed to extend my domain and develop more efficient methods.

"This was when I discovered children. Mind you, there were technical problems to surmount. They were easy enough to harvest, but their pain tolerances are too low; you can't really get fancy with them. They die too easily. But they're the heart of the family and that's the heart of the herd. Take them and you rip the fiercest bond of the species. Wouldn't you agree, Father? Father? Oh, I'll go on. I know you're out there.

"Children, their innocence makes them so easy to seduce. There's no end to the supply. But it isn't really them I'm after at this point. Oh, I know there's something in their purity and innocence that makes destroying them like pissing in the temple — destroying the holy of holies. But it's those silent parents out there. Those wishes, dreams, so fiercely held that I was after. Think of it. Each death radiating out in a lattice of guilt and rage, fear and sorrow without end. This would be my kingdom: pain everlasting. Long after the flesh has failed to transmit my message, the soul goes on. Such efficiency, such breadth of scope. I had found the solution to my aging, a legacy that would go on forever beyond me. To legend, to myth. The missing ones like black holes torn in the fabric of families. Around the edges, as close as they dare to get they would embroider stories, lessons, signposts to their children and their children's children to avoid that place. I would leave a mark on all those lives for generations. As long as there was memory, I would be there. In each and every house. *Whew*. My goodness. Well, I feel so much better, Father, let me tell you, having gotten that off my chest. This was the right thing to do. I was ready to share my creation with another. What do you think, Father? No. Don't answer that. Give it some thought. Hell of a tale, isn't it? I'm taking my show on the road these days. You know — revisiting the scenes of some of my greatest triumphs, my earlier crops, to see what has come up after all these years.

"Thanks for the talk. It's been a pleasure. You probably saved a life today. Who knows? I'll be back. This confession stuff is exhausting. We'll talk about a suitable penance next time. Some Hail Marys, okay?"

"That won't . . ." Father Shannon snarled.

"Listen, I want to come back. I mean I really want to seek God's forgiveness. Can I come back tomorrow, huh? What do you say?"

"You may come back."

Father Shannon was surprised at his feelings. His hands were clutching his knees and his teeth hurt. He heard the other door open and close. For reasons he could not fathom, nor truth be told did he want to, Father Shannon opened his door to the booth and went quickly out of the church. He saw the stranger striding swiftly away, heading toward the only house at the end of Point Repulse whistling in the late afternoon sun like you or me.

Chapter 8

ANYONE WHO DOESN'T BELIEVE IN ENTROPY ISN'T DOING HIS OWN laundry. I mean, where the hell do all those socks go? I stuck my head in the dryer, looking up and all around. The black holes of the universe are filled with solitary socks looking through eternity for their mates. The universe is coming apart at a rate equal to the number of socks lost per load. Believe it.

I pulled my head out, waved bye-bye to my latest lost foot-wear, and went back to the bedroom to find a new pair of socks. I slipped them on and then my Bally loafers. I stood in front of the mirror silently thanking John Weitz for making stylish clothes for a size 48 regular with .45 caliber underarm deodorant. Navy blue suit, white shirt, rep tie. Rebellion in colored jockey shorts. I passed muster and went out to my car.

I would rather have waited until night to see Lester, but my best chance of getting past his security was in the after-noon lull before one of his shows. I pulled up onto the Beltway and headed out to Potomac: Bethesda's bigger, richer brother; the flashiest address in suburban Washington, "Megabucks City." Home to orthodontists, bankers, paper chase lawyers, and the longest running whips-and-chains show in the area.

I hadn't seen Lester Kroll in over two years, but I heard from him regularly: invitations to his Halloween party each year that I always declined. I'd done some work for Lester keeping his good name unsullied. He'd lied to me up the kazoo. When I'd sorted out what was what, I was ready to hang Lester out to dry. However, a lot of not-so-innocent people would have joined him. I didn't do that, and that left Lester very worried about me. He couldn't understand not exploiting a weakness, and behavior he can't understand worries him. So the invitations came regularly. I never went out there for his S & M smorgasbord. The VCR version would be out the next day. No thanks. Once is too much. But if anyone knew the heart and soul of Washington's latex underworld, Lester did. He'd know who our canine commandant was, if anyone would. It was worth a try, at least.

I got off at River Road and headed west. Past Burning Tree: "The President's Country Club." Past the Deutsche Schule, through the old village square toward Seneca. The last time I'd been up this way had been to pick thornless blackberries, hung up on trellises. A man-made pleasure now, delivered without the back breaking, finger pricking work nature first demanded for it. I hoped tonight would go as easily, but I doubted it.

I pulled my car to the side of the road and looked at my watch. It was a little after two P.M. I wanted to go in with a caravan of cars. Pretty soon a pair of Mercedes, a Porsche, and a Datsun 280Z rolled through. I joined the parade. The stone archway had a brass nameplate: Count Aleksandr Karoly—also known by a lucky few as Lester Kroll of Pump City, Alabama.

I parked in the corner and waited for the others to get out and head in. Tires squealed in the driveway and a car slewed into the lot. All heads turned.

If there'd been a cherry on the roof of the car you'd have seen the fastest convening of the American Amnesia Society on record. The car pulled up next to me. There was a girl inside, alone. She turned to look at me for a second. Her hair was pulled up into a pony tail on the top of her head. Her eyes were rimmed in black and silver makeup. Small crystalline tears of makeup dripped from each eye. She was one of the girls Lester had on hand at the house so that there would never be any permutations that would go unrealized. She was grabbing a bag from the back seat. I slid across my seat. She opened her car door and started to slide out. I opened mine and wedged it against hers and got out to talk to her.

"What's the matter with you, asshole? Why don't you close your door, dammit." She tried to squirm out and suddenly lurched to her right. "Oh fuck! I broke one of my heels. You stupid shit. You know what these cost?"

I slid out of my car and stood between her and the house. "Listen, I just want to—"

"I don't give a damn what you want." She looked up at my face. "Christ, what's the matter with you. There's plenty to get inside. You don't need to get physical out here. Listen, let me go, dammit. I'm late and the count will really be pissed."

I didn't move. "Wait a minute."

She gritted her teeth. "If he comes out here looking for me and I tell him you wouldn't let me in, Kurt will fuck you up good. So you better let me go, Mister. I mean it."

"No. You listen a minute. I don't want to do anything to you, with you, or near you. But I do want to see the count and I don't think he will want to see me. All I want for you to do is let me in with you when you go in. After that I'll deal with Kurt and the count."

"Oh yeah, right. Kurt would kill you."

"Listen, sweetheart—and I know you won't believe this—but the last time Kurt was short with me it took three months to rebuild him. So don't use Kurt to scare me."

"What are you gonna to do? Kill him? Man, I don't want no part of this. Let me out of here." She tried to back away from me. I grabbed her wrists. She dropped her bag.

"I'm not going to do anything unless the count pisses me off. I just want to talk with him, and you're going to help me do that. Right?" I was tired of this clenched teeth chatter and wished she'd just do it my way.

"All right, all right. Just get off of me, you big ape. I'll let you in. You just have to promise me that you won't tell the count I did it. He'd kill me. I mean it. Have you ever seen him when he gets mad? Christ. He's a crazy man."

"Your secret will die with me. Let's go." I leaned back, and she tried to kick me and run for it. Running on one five-inch spike heel is no mean feat. I reached and grabbed her around her corseted waist and clapped a hand over her mouth. "Look, goddammit, there may be lives at stake here, kids' lives. Lester knows something. That's all I want. Just a talk and I'll be gone. If that means anything to you stop squirming and nod your head. Otherwise you spend the night in my trunk and I go in and do it the hard way. I'll be sure to tell Lester you were a great help." This whole thing was beginning to go sour on me, and I was starting to wish Arnie Kendall was here. Point him in the right direction and get out of the way. You can always reason with the survivors.

She calmed down. I spread my fingers open a little. She whispered, "All right, I'll do it. No tricks. Honest. I promise."

"You'd better, sugar. Next trick is you last. My normal jovial mood is about all used up. Got it?"

She nodded.

I put her down. She reached down and plucked off her outrageous shoes and threw them in the woods. "Shit. There goes fifty bucks." She was wearing fishnet stockings attached to a black leather teddy, open to her waist; thick leather brace-lets on her wrists; and a collar around her neck.

"All right, Little Mary Sunshine, let's go." I followed her around the back of the house to a windowless door with a punch code lock on it. I slipped my arm through hers, pulled her close, and looked her square in the eyes. "Do it my way and everything will go fine. You'll go your way and I'll go mine. You tell Lester I'm in the house and I'll tell him you let me in. Fair enough?"

She slipped her tongue out of her mouth and licked her

lips. "Will you come see me inside? I'm in room six."

"Sure thing, blossom. Wouldn't miss it. We can talk about old times. Let's go."

She tried to nibble my ear and wrapped a leg around mine. Love with an anaconda. I didn't know if being rough turned her on or this was a last-ditch effort to avoid going in, but I'd had it with little Miss Muffett. I grabbed her right arm by the elbow with enough force to numb her hand. "Stop it. You're hurting me!"

"Sorry. How gauche of me. Punch the code." She tapped out the code with her inch long nails. The door slid silently open to a dark corridor. I'd never been in this part of the house. I dragged the girl along with me. The first room on the left was full of toys. I pulled my friend into it. Among many other things there was a gag lying on the bed and rows of leashes on pegs on the wall. I pulled down a leash and clipped it to her collar. Then the gag. She looked at it and at me and back at it. "I wanted to trust you, but you've been a real disappointment so far."

"I won't scream. I promise."

"With this on, I know you won't. Open up."

She licked her lips again slowly as she opened her mouth. Her tongue licked the gag as it went in. I put the gag in and tightened it around her head, grabbed the leash, and went looking for Lester. I wanted to be done with chores as soon as possible. Maybe if I soaked in Lysol I'd feel better after this. I think my friend was having a lot more fun than I was.

We left the room and headed toward the light. One thing, we wouldn't stand out in this crowd. Just a man and his girl out for a stroll. A couple passed us in the hall. The woman dug her spurs in, pulled up on the bit, struck the man with her crop, and he winced and cantered off. Humpalong Cassidy, my boyhood hero. Two main playrooms branched off on either side. There was enough rubber and plastic worn in those rooms to be Playtex's profit margin for the year. A shtupperware party from Fredericks of Dachau. My reluctant playmate gargled behind her gag. I unsnapped it and pulled her close to me. "Yes?"

"These are the orgy rooms. The private rooms are downstairs; Alex is probably up in his room upstairs."

"Why are you telling me this?"

"Because the damn gag hurts and if you're not going to fuck me, it ain't worth it."

Upstairs would be where Lester videotaped the private rooms. That gave him the leverage to stay open untouched for as long as he had. I'd learned that when Lester had tried to set me up to flush out the overeager editor who'd pocketed a copy of a tape. That was when I'd met Kurt.

A shadow closed off the hall for a second. The bouncy, slightly zigzag gait was all too familiar. I pulled my friend close to me and kissed her, harder than I had too. She tried to climb right up my body the way a drowning person does. We conversed tongue in cheek for a moment. The shadow passed on.

She licked her lips. "Um. Yum. Nice tongue. I bet you give good head."

"Yeah, I'm a cunning linguist. Let's go upstairs."

I pocketed the gag and tried to take the leash off and hold her hand. She didn't want me to. I gave up. We went up the stairs. I heard the bathroom to the left gargling. Kurt's ablutions?

"Which room is Lester's?"

She pointed down the hall to the right. "Okay. Thanks. Now disappear. I told you I'd keep you out of it. Scoot."

"Okay. If Kurt doesn't kill you, come see me in room six. I'll be in the trapeze."

"Sure thing." Just doing her practi-cum in American Fucklore: "The erotic uses of the trapeze, swing, and teeter-totter" by Jungle Jim. She turned away, then back.

"Why do you keep calling Alex, Lester?"

"Because the count is really Lester Kroll of Pump City, Alabama. Remember that. Now begone!"

I turned and glided down the hall. I heard Lester's wheezy bark of a laugh. Jabba the Hutt lives. The door was unlocked. I palmed the knob and rolled in behind it. Lester sat behind his console: eight screens showing the best in suburban horseplay. Lester hadn't changed. Cadaverously thin, his oversized head with its whipped cream pompadour and fish eyes bracing a banana nose made you want to laugh at him. His downswept shark's mouth said don't. He was as cuddly as an ice pick.

"Hello, Lester."

He spun about. "What the hell? How'd you get in? What're you doing here?" His hands flashed for a button on the console. I grabbed his bony wrists and pinned them together. As I spoke, I rubbed his wrist bones against each other — just to assure his attention.

"Lester, Lester. I've never braced you before so you know I wouldn't be here if I didn't have a good reason. I could give a shit about what goes on here. I also know you're historically uncooperative, and I have neither time nor patience nor money to wine and dine this information out of you. So be helpful and I'll be gone. Don't make it harder on yourself than it has to be."

I played bone grinder again, and he yelped. "Okay, okay."

I dropped his hands. He rubbed his wrists slowly. "Good, Lester. I'm glad we understand each other."

His eyes dimmed. Manhole covers of the soul. "Don't call me that again, Haggerty, or Kurt will throw you out."

"Lester, if Kurt even lets his shadow land on me I'll leave him in worse shape than Humpty Dumpty."

"Is that a threat, little man?" Kurt was in the doorway. I rose to meet him.

"No threat, Kurt. It's a promise." He was an average size specimen of his kind: six foot three, two hundred forty pounds.

Just big enough to palm me if he wanted to. He was blocky through his red jumpsuit with the big lifter's belt cinched tight. His full red beard flared out. A Santa Claus with a hostile streak the size of an interstate highway. Like always, he leaned forward as if he was walking into a wind. He was bobbing from side to side. A cobra's dance before it strikes. I grew fists.

"That's enough. I don't want a fight here." Lester looked at me. "At least not now. Be warned, Haggerty. I owe you this one for keeping your mouth shut without ever tapping me, but this is the end of the gravy train. Come around me again, ever, for any reason, and I will let Kurt do anything he wants with you. Anything."

Kurt smiled.

"Fair enough, Lester, uh, count." I smiled with contempt.

"Kurt, leave us here for thirty minutes. If Mr. Haggerty is still here at that time, dispose of him as you see fit. Also, check all the doors and the security. I want to know how he got in."

"Tina said she saw him go upstairs. That's why I came up." Kurt turned to leave, and I blew him a kiss.

"What do you want, Haggerty? Make it quick. I've got a lot going on I don't want to miss."

Lester's body looked like the logical adaptation for a voyeur: all his sense organs enlarged and dead from the neck down.

"I want to know about a guy who uses a—"

"Shush. Wait a minute. Oh boy. Look at this." He waved at me over his shoulder without turning from the bank of screens. They looked like the composite eyes of a giant insect. A locust of lust harvesting all those images, stripping all those people down to chaff. I glanced at screen six. My little friend was busy, very busy. She had her hands full. And her mouth and just about everywhere else. She looked like La Guardia with all her bays full and incoming stacked up all around. It was a crime of passion, your honor. A crime of passion. Not a plea, but an accusation.

"Look, look. See her, she's a justice department lawyer. Look at this, look!" I thought Lester was going to levitate out of his seat. A woman was walking across one of the main playrooms. She strode purposefully in the full battle regalia of her nakedness and then knelt in the middle of the room. The other women in the room approached her. They bound her hands behind her back and shackled them to her ankles. I tried to look elsewhere, but the images were all the same. I was truly in the crotch of the universe. One of the women reappeared with a leather hood that was pulled down over the bound woman's head so that it covered her eyes. It was adjusted and then two black plugs were inserted into her nostrils. She opened her mouth to breathe. Men began to line up masturbating. I punched some buttons on the console. The screen went black.

"Listen Lester—"

"No, you listen. You come in here. You break in here," he pointed his finger at me, "and run around telling me what to do. Okay, I'll answer your questions, but we do it my way, Haggerty. My way. You just sit and wait."

Lester leaned back and punched another button; the images reappeared. "Mary, bring me a bourbon straight up. You want anything?" I remembered when touring foreign countries, don't drink the water.

"No thanks."

Lester leaned back at his console, comand center of the S.S. *Pornucopia*. I looked for some place to sit.

"You know this is the best setup I've ever had. Here in D.C. is better than L.A., better than New York. You can't hurt me, Haggerty. You can't touch me. I'm untouchable. I've got everybody I need in my pocket. I'm talking to you because I want to. You couldn't make me. You're a nobody, Haggerty. A nothing. I could have you dropped off the Cabin John Bridge with two phone calls. One to bury you and the other to cover it up. You're a nuisance, and tonight's a night I don't want messed up. So we'll have our talk, but we'll do it my way."

I hoped all this bluster made Lester feel better about talking to me.

"You know why I'm so solid here? I bet you don't. That's because you're just a stupid dick, Haggerty. No imagination. No flair. I'm so solid here because this town's so perfect for what I've got to sell. What do they make in this town, huh Haggerty, tell me?"

"I don't know. What do they make, Lester?" I shrugged my shoulders. I felt like my father was trying to teach me arithmetic. I was getting stupider by the minute.

"They make rules, laws, here. That's what. This city oozes power, man. Real power. Power to do things your own way. You know what that does?"

Lesson two. I took out my pad and pencil. "No, Lester, tell me. What does that mean?"

There was a knock at the door. "Come in." Mary, Mary not at all contrary entered. She had on an apron that once was a butterfly's wings and spike heels that would break your orthopedist's heart. She curtsied, and Lester goosed her. "Thank you, m'lord." She squatted on Lester's hand for a minute and then he excused her.

"Where was I?"

"Fingering the help, Lester. Let's finish the lecture. I'm getting older by the minute."

"Patience, Haggerty. Or I'll have to start all over again. Wouldn't want that, would we?"

No, wouldn't want that, Sister Benigna, chief penguin at the primary school. I don't want to start all over writing 'I will not talk in class' five hundred times because I didn't dot the *i*. No ma'am. You heartless cunt.

"What this city is, is a magnet for the power hungry. Only the winners get here. They're used to getting their way, getting to the top. Very driven people. But this is a very frustrating town. Democracy's like that. Everybody has a say. Checks and balances, procedural safeguards, rules, rights, 'justice for all.' Very frustrating, always compromising, having to hear the other side. It's hard being that close to all that power and not being able to freely use it.

"This is a hard town to be frustrated in, too. Not like L.A. or New York. There's power there in those towns, too, but a different sort. Image power, but all kinds of images can exist in those towns. Any town that can tolerate 42nd Street in daylight has no need of me. There's image power at work here, too, but it's a lot less free here. You represent America: America as your cud-chewing constituents in Horseplop, North Dakota, want to see themselves; America the beautiful, home of the brave, land of the free. You're always aware of the media, the need for that iamge at all times to be what all the yokels back home want you to be.

"But you're here; there's all this power humming in the air. A free-flow energy field, if you can only tap it. And you're here because you love power. But it's so frustrating and you can't show that. Not in public. See how it comes together. I got a whiff of this town and knew this was where I'd settle down. We're custom-made for each other. All those power-hungry, frustrated, driven bastards needing a place to shuck their respectable images and purge themselves. Hell, I'm a social service agency. I offer release and privacy. What do you think would happen if all that tension couldn't find an outlet?

"That's what I am: a safety valve for America. Defusing all those potential explosions on the Hill that could lead our country to ruin. A lot of high-powered cocks have gotten relieved here. You know why I'm out here in Potomac and you're sucking shit somewhere on the streets, Haggerty? Because I've got imagination. I knew what this town needed. I could sense it. You, you follow pissant dreams for nickels and dimes. You're going nowhere."

"Are we done, Lester? Any more and I won't have enough self-respect to talk to you, and that's why I'm here."

"Yeah, yeah, ask away and let me go back to business."

"I'm looking for a girl and through her a guy. All I've got is a loop. It's homemade with a dominance shtick. Guy was into a nasty dog-training routine. Girl had real close-cropped blond hair, blue eyes, no tattoos or scars—I looked. The tape's probably at least four years old. What can you tell me?"

"I can tell you to get lost, Leo, but you wouldn't, would you? You'd nose around and make trouble. Even if you couldn't close me down officially, you'd scare my clients off, ruin my reputation for privacy. You and that thing of yours. What was his name?"

"Arnie, Arnie Kendall."

"Yeah, that's right. You know I tried to buy him afterward. I wanted him to cripple you. He turned me down cold. You'd just come back with him, wouldn't you? You really surprised me. I thought I could use you as a bird dog then buy you off or scare you off when this was all over. But neither Kurt nor Erica worked, did they? You turned out to be one persistent motherfucker. I thought you were just stupid. Oh well, live and learn."

I knew Lester would eventually give me what I wanted, but first he had to rebuild his ego, make it look like he was doing me a favor, not doing what he was told to do. "What about Captain K-9 and blondie?"

"This requires a lot of discretion, Leo. Very sensitive information. But then I know that about you, too. Persistent and private. A man who can keep a secret. I am surprised you've never tried to touch me up before."

"Why should I? I told you I wouldn't. You were a client. I don't like your business, but I've seen worse. Everybody's here because they want to be. They play funny games, but then, so's cricket."

"I tolerate your existence because you've been so discreet.

I could have you taken out. But then there's Arnie. He'd know right where to look. You've proven not to be worth the trouble to remove. But I'm not used to living so long 'cooperatively' with another person. I don't like the anxiety of it at all. The simplicity of removal is too attractive. Now here you are reminding me that I must tolerate you, and I have to ask myself, why?"

"I'm building your character, Lester. That's what anxiety tolerance is: maturity, knowing when to hold on and when to let go. You'll be a better man for the experience. Trust me. Call it 'therapeutic parasitism.' I'm a hard lesson to learn, but I'm even harder to ignore. Apart from that, you're not a killer. You can cover up this foolishness, but murder's serious work and you're a jester. A joker, but not a killer. Kurt, yes, but he's like an android. Until you wind him up and point him in the right direction, he'll sleep or behead cats or do whatever amuses him. No animating intelligence. I haven't proven worth it and, if anything, you're an expedient man, Lester. That I know about you. Easy way out if there is one. In this case, tell me a story about Goldilocks and the Dog-man and I'll be gone like a bad dream."

"Okay, okay. Goldilocks, as you like to call her, was a girl who worked for me. She also did some freelance work on the side. Well, we got a call from her. This was about seven, seven and half years ago. She was barely able to talk, but told us where she was and that she needed help. She'd been hurt by a trick. So I sent Kurt over with our house doctor. Excitement leads to bad judgment and we have injuries now and then." Lester shrugged his shoulders. "You walk a tight-rope, you're gonna fall. What can I say?"

When the sideshow's in the big top you got trouble. "Close the circus, Lester, but what do I know? No imagination, right?"

"Anyway, Kurt went out there. It was a mess. The doctor did what he could there. They brought her back here. She stayed here for a while, until she healed up. Some things we couldn't fix. Anyway, she retired from this business after that. I don't know what she's doing now. The reason I know she's the girl is she's blond, looks like a dyke, and used to talk now and then about some of her tricks — the girls all do — including a strange guy who had a doggie routine he made her do. Maybe he did it to her, maybe not. She never said which john did it. Just told Kurt that the john had flipped out, gone nuts on her. The 'play' was no longer enough. He'd gotten a taste of blood and liked it. All this here is 'theatre.' Bedtime stories for bad boys and girls.

"Everyone's here because they want to play at being bad and being punished. You see, you can't really hurt someone who wants to be. The victims let you hurt them. Hurting someone only counts if they don't want it. So it's all a charade here. The real McCoy is for those who can't be satisfied by the play. It's a failure of imagination, of fantasy. The ones who need the real thing are out beyond this little playhouse. Maybe your friend, the dogman, took a trip to the great beyond, and once you go there, the 'play' is never enough again. You've got to have headier thrills all the time. Maybe that's where the dogman is, pursuing newer depths of pleasure. A solitary explorer of his own limits. Anyway, Goldilocks got hurt real bad by a man who went into the wild blue yonder, and she also was seeing a man who used a routine like you describe."

"The name, Lester, name and address."

"I'll call to let her know who you are and that I say you're okay to talk to. She doesn't meet men alone anymore at all. Whatever that guy did freaked her out. She's been a recluse ever since. I won't tell her what you want because I don't think she'd talk to you. She never talked further about that night to anyone."

"Okay. Make your call."

Lester spun away and punched the number on the phone.

He looked up and changed the focus on one of the monitors and let out a low whistle.

"Ingrid. This is Alexy. Is Jocelyn there? Good. I want to send a man over who wants to talk to her. Yeah, he's okay. I vouch for him completely. Okay? That's a dear, good. No. He won't touch her. It's not business. Yes, I know. I know. He just wants to talk with her. Okay. I'll ask." He cupped his hand over the mouthpiece. "Her roommate wants to be there when you talk to her, otherwise it's no go. All right?"

"Yeah, fine."

"Okay. He says that's fine. When are you going to go over?" he asked me.

"Right now, if she'll see me. Otherwise as soon as possible."

"How about now, Ingrid? Okay. Yeah, he'll be there in about thirty or forty minutes. Name's Leo Haggerty. About six feet, two hundred pounds, brown on brown, cookie duster . . ."

I took off my jacket, turned my arm over, and pointed to my elbow.

"Big horseshoe scar outside of the left elbow. Okay? Fine." Lester hung up and wrote the address on a piece of paper, tore it off, and handed it to me.

"Here, meeting is adjourned. Don't make this a habit, Leo. I just might decide to test how tough you really are."

"Ta-ta, Lester. Believe me, I hope I never have to see you again, too. I'll let myself out."

"Use the back door."

I turned to leave, and Lester was on the intercom, "Kurt, please escort our guest out. Now."

I shrugged my shoulders. "That's unnecessary, Lester, really."

Kurt materialized like a lost hope and smiled at me. "Let's go. Move it."

Chapter 9

JOCELYN AND INGRID LIVED IN GEORGETOWN, IN ONE OF THE old row houses on 38th above the University. I pushed the buzzer on the pebbled glass and wrought iron door. A voice came over the intercom. "Yes?"

"This is Leo Haggerty. Lester Kroll, uh Count Karoly, called and said I was coming."

"Step into the vestibule."

The door clicked. I turned the handle and stepped into an airlock foyer. The door behind me locked again. A ceiling camera scanned me like a lab animal. "Roll up your sleeve."

I did and rolled my elbow over. The nasty keloid horseshoe was slick and rubbery. Courtesy of a twelve-year-old's rainy day handlebar header into a culvert.

"Unlock the door."

I stepped into another foyer. Ingrid, I presumed, stood halfway up the stairs. Her round face was without edges or bones, streaked blond hair piled on her head like a soft golden ice cream cone. Her eyes were lavender and as direct as lasers.

"Are you one of the count's cronies?" Her slightest sneer tipped the scales, and I let the truth tumble out.

"Not by a long shot. He owes me a favor. That's why he told me how to find you, or rather, Jocelyn."

"What kind of favor?" Hands on hip.

"One time I didn't bring his whole house down when I could have."

"Too bad. What do you want with Jocelyn?"

"I'm a private detective, looking for a missing person. I believe Jocelyn once knew a man who can lead me to that person."

She didn't look impressed. "How do you know that?"

"I understand that she was hurt once by a man. Beaten up. It's that man I want to find."

"Good bye, Mr. Haggerty. We have nothing to discuss." She turned abruptly and began to climb the stairs.

"Wait a minute. Hold on. I don't know what happened back then, but there could be lives at stake here. Children's lives."

Ingrid turned slowly and spoke slower still. "There is a life at stake here, Mr. Haggerty. A very painfully rebuilt life. One whose core your questions threaten. I will not let that happen. Leave now." A Beretta's round black snout punctuated our discussion. Period. The end.

"Okay, I'll leave. I don't know what you are to Jocelyn. You sound like her keeper, not her friend. But I'll be back. One way or another, I'll have my talk. You can't keep the world away forever, and I am persistent. Know that. I don't want this to be an ordeal. But two small girls' lives and possibly their father's ride on my finding the man who I believe hurt your friend. You can stay and watch everything. Christ, I don't want to hurt your friend at all if I can help it. But she's the only lead we've got, and I just can't pass it by."

"I'm sorry, Mr. Haggerty. But it's just not possible. You see —"

"Inky. What's going on. Who's here?" A tremulous voice in the dark.

"Jocelyn, my name is Leo Haggerty. I need to talk with you very badly. It's very important. If I could just have a few minutes of your time."

Jocelyn came down out of the shadows. She was tall and thin, almost anorectic. She wore a black and white mid-calf skirt and crisp white ironing board blouse with a shoestring tie. Her face was utterly without lines and almost entirely covered with makeup, a white pancake with splotches of color. Her video blond hair, now black, fell on her shoulders like rain. She stepped slowly down the stairs, past Ingrid, who put a hand on her shoulders. "You don't want to talk to this man, Jocelyn. He wants to talk about that night."

"Miss—I don't know your name."

"Drake."

"Miss Drake, I don't want to cause you any upset about whatever happened to you, but I do want to know anything about the man who hurt you. It's terribly important."

"I really don't remember anything at all about that night. I'm sure I can't be of any help."

"Well, perhaps we don't need to talk about that night. Had you ever been with that man before?"

"Really Jocelyn, you know this isn't good for you." Ingrid's grip grew tighter on Jocelyn's shoulder. If looks could kill, she's have been the gorgon of Georgetown.

Jocelyn looked up, "Yes. You're right. Go away. That's my past. It's over. I don't want to talk about it. I just don't care. Leave me alone. All of you."

"You can't just walk away from it. It goes with you everywhere. It's why you're holed up in this house. Whoever hurt you will hurt others. I think he already has, and I'm trying to stop that before it goes on and there are more scared people like you who's lives he's played havoc with."

She turned on the staircase and bent at the waist, her white knuckled hands gripped the railing. Through clenched teeth the words fell out slowly, like bricks of despair. "Leave me be. Go away. I have forgotten that night. It's all gone. I can't go back there. I won't." Ingrid looked ready to gut and filet me.

"You let the bastard win then. You may be alive, but you ain't livin'."

"Don't you say that. You don't know. I'm doing all the living I can."

"He's got you holed up in this dark corner of the world, and he walks in the sunlight."

"Who cares about the sunlight?" she barked hoarsely. "That's my price for living. Don't you know? That's why he let me live. He fixed me good." She put her hand to her face and when it came away, so did her left eye. She held it out to me. "That's why I'm alive. Here. Take it, you bastard. It's my good one."

It was hard to look at her lopsided face. "Please help me bring him down. Before he does this to anyone else. Fight back. If you couldn't then, do it now."

She slipped the eye back in. "It's too late. Don't you see, it's too late. I have my life. It's what I have. I won't upset that for anyone. Not even your guilt trip. It's all I have left. I escaped. I'm alive. It's what he left me. What he gave me. I don't have anything else. I escaped my past, my memories. They're gone, thank God." She sat down on the steps. Her legs were in the light, her face in my shadows.

"There's nothing to fight for. This is what he left me with. He took everything else that night. Everything. You say fight. I fought. I begged. I pleaded. It didn't matter. Nothing mattered. He did what he wanted."

She slowly stood up. "Don't you tell me how much living I'm doing. You don't know what it took to get this far. Well, I'm not giving this up for nobody. Nobody. I'm sorry. I'd really like to help, but I can't. I really can't, mister. It just takes too much, and I don't have it left to give. I'm all used up."

"All right. I'll go. If we find him and catch him, do you want to know? I'll let you know. I promise."

"I don't know. Just let me be. Go."

I went back to my car. My brain felt like whipped shit. I was going to have to tell DeVito about her. He might not get anything more from her, and he might do her more harm than good. And then again, he might get a lead that would save a life. And then if we knew how things would turn out we'd all live forever.

Most of us die in little pieces, our illusions go first, then our dreams, then our stamina, and we just come to a halt. For some, death visits in a firestorm and there's no time to accommodate, to make the best of it. If the blasted stump survives at all, blackened and twisted, the shape it takes is usually beyond control. If you're lucky, life is a holding action. Cutting our losses, pruning back what we've lost to preserve what we've got. There's no way out but through. First the bad news. Then the good news. While it's a hell of a trip, straight ahead is the shortest route.

I pulled my collar up and slid into the car. I had no place to go. Nobody to see but my office. I drove to a phone booth and called my answering service. Maggie Saunders had called. Twice. I ought to check in with her. She probably shouldn't be alone at this time. I dialed her number.

"Hello, Mrs. Saunders?"

"Yes." Her voice was tight with anticipation.

"This is Leo Haggerty. I'd like to stop by and fill you in on my progress and ask a few more questions, if it's not too late."

"Please do. No, it's not too late." She laughed bitterly, "I hope it's not at least."

"I'll be there in about half an hour, okay?"

"Fine, Mr. Haggerty, have you eaten, by the way?"

"No, I haven't."

"Would you care to eat here? I hate to eat alone. Frankly, I've done that too often in my life."

"Thank you. That would be very nice."

"What do you like?"

"Anything and everything. I'll see you shortly."

Hanging up I looked up at the late afternoon sky. When I was young I'd lie on the front lawn and look up at the twinkling darkness and try to imagine the universe's end beyond the stars. And then what was outside that and when that ended, what was there and so on without end. I remembered a friend of mine showing me that if you put two mirrors facing each other and looked into the infinite regress of your image, just as you are about to behold infinity your head gets in the way. We're God's idiot children in quarantine here. Just on the cusp of consciousness, evolved enough to ask the right questions, but unable to grasp the answers.

Chapter 10

THE FRONT LIGHTS WERE ON IN THE SAUNDERS' HOUSE. I WENT up and knocked on the door. Mrs. Saunders let me in. I had my case notes with me and still no appetite. The dining room table was set.

"Would you care to eat first, Mr. Haggerty?"

"That would be fine. Thank you, Mrs. Saunders." I felt terribly stiff and formal, like I was visiting one of my maiden aunts — the ones that cleaned house for fun.

I sat at one end of the table, probably in Herb Saunders' place, and Mrs. Saunders went into the kitchen. I was getting very edgy.

Mrs. Saunders returned with a piece of baked chicken, mashed potatoes, and a small caesar salad.

"What would you like to drink?"

"Ice water would be fine. Coffee later, if that's okay."

"It's already set up." She left and came back with a matching meal. We ate in silence. Again like at my aunt's, I detuned my inhaler from 78 to 33 ⅓. Not eating frequently with other people, I tend to feed rather than dine, and I'm usually done inside of five minutes. I try to slow down when I'm with others. Leaving them to finish alone make them edgy. Dinner ended in a photofinish, a simultaneous orgasm of good manners.

"Thank you. That was very nice." There had been very little conversation during dinner. The only real things to talk about were absolute appetite suppressants so we held them at bay until we finished.

"It was. I hate to eat alone and I won't cook for myself. It was nice to have company. Would you like that coffee now?"

"Please." When she left I got my folder, pulled out my notes, and went through my questions. I realized I had very few and didn't even know why I was here.

Maggie Saunders returned. I looked at my notes trying to find something to ask her. There wasn't much. But then again I told her I'd call if I had any news. I thought I'd round-about it. She might not even want to know. Prolonged suffering teaches you to have respect for your defenses. That's all that's between us and night never ending.

"I've helped flesh out a lead for Sergeant DeVito." Which reminded me I needed to call him. "Do you want to know about it?"

"Frankly, no. I'm very cautious. I don't want to get my hopes up. The disappointment is just too much. I learned that early on." A shudder passed through her.

"It sounds like your husband could never do that."

"I think that's true. Herb could never let go of anything. He courted me as if he was running a marathon. He just kept up the pace until I gave in. Mind you, I'm not complaining. I needed the pursuit. I said yes when I'd gotten enough of it."

She sipped her coffee. "You know when you described yourself on the phone as persistent and imaginative, it occurred to me that that's how I'd describe Herb. He can be driven and creative, but now he's only making demons. He just can't turn the engine off. I know that. He doesn't know how to rest."

"How about you? You said you lived to take care of your children and husband. And as your guest, I would say you did that well. How about yourself?"

She touched her mouth. "How about me. How about me." As she repeated the phrase the inflection changed, a slight rotation of meaning, as if she were checking the facets of an alien crystal. "I can let go of things. I have always been able to. I'm always prepared to. Secretly I know things won't work out. It's never if, but when."

"Have you let go of this?"

She bowed her head as if she were praying. "I could never tell Herb this. I don't know if I could ever tell myself this, but yes, I've let go. The girls are dead. I know it in my heart. I couldn't carry the burden Herb does, and I know he'd never understand that. It would have cost us our marriage if I'd told him. So I just grieved silently for them. I'm not sure now whether we aren't as far apart as we'd have been if I'd have told him. But I still have him to care for and I love him. And he does love me, as he knows me."

She looked at me. "I don't know why I told you that. I guess I've needed to say that to someone for a long time. And in some ways, you remind me of Herb. It's probably as close as I'll ever get to telling him. Maybe that's why I asked you here tonight. I don't know."

"Maybe that's why I came," I offered.

"Anyway, thank you for listening." Her eyes were bright and wet.

I started to get very uncomfortable again. "Listen, let me call DeVito up. He'll want to know what I found."

"Okay. I'll go into the kitchen to get dessert. Is pie okay?"

"Sure. Fine."

I pushed away from the table and went into the living room, sinking into the recliner. I put the phone in my lap. When it rang, DeVito growled a greeting. "Yeah."

"Sergeant DeVito? This is Leo Haggerty. Listen. I, uh, wanted to . . ." a new thought popped up. "To ask you about something you'd said before about Saunders. You said he hadn't sounded like this in years. Not since something."

"Yeah. The kooks and weirdos. The crazy letters and calls. He'd get all churned up, but he was also drinking a lot back then. That's when he sounded like that letter."

"Okay. Thanks. I'll let you know if I turn up anything."

That lie didn't set well with me, but I thought Jocelyn Drake might get a little peace out of it, for now.

"Mrs. Saunders, you said there was no alcohol in the house. Did you check the house thoroughly and the trash?"

"Yes. I knew all of Herb's hiding places."

I pulled out the letter and reread it. He said the Devil spoke today. Perhaps a kook, but not one with a theory on how to find the girls, but the one who took them. He spoke to him. How? Not in person. He'd be in pieces everywhere. How then? Mail? Telephone?

"When you went to work yesterday, had the mail arrived?"

"Yes, It comes early here."

"Anything for Herb?"

"No. Just the usual junk and coupons. I went through it all at work and tossed it out. Why?"

Maybe Herb's letter wasn't the result of Jack Daniels' amnesia mouthwash. Maybe he did speak to the kidnapper by phone. How to trace it? If it was long distance, there'd be a record—if not a tap—perhaps.

"Was there a trace put on your phones?"

"Oh yes, right away. It was on for a long time. We got so many calls. I think it's still on. Why?"

"Don't ask. You don't want to know." I started to get that unscratchable itch of desire. Something emerging, coalescing just beyond my reach. Come on, baby, come clean. I called the phone company security and asked for a supervisor.

"Yes. This is Mrs. Ramsey. May I help you?"

"I hope so. My name is Leo Haggerty. I'm a private detective, and I'd like to know if the tap on the Herbert Saunders' line is still on?"

"That's very curious. That's the second inquiry we've gotten in two days on that trace, after all this time. Yes, it's still on, but we already turned the information on the call over to the police."

That's what you think, sister. Ho ho ho, Merry Christmas.

He called, and Saunders got the number and traced it. I thanked her, hung up, and called DeVito back.

"Listen, Pete, I think whoever took the girls called Saunders yesterday. Saunders somehow got the information off the trace from the security office and he's after whoever called."

"What the hell?"

"Listen. Who has access to the trace information?"

"I do. I'm officer in charge."

"Well, call phone security and I'll bet you dollars to donuts you were given the information on the calls. Go ahead."

"All right. I'll call you right back. Where are you at?"

"I'm at the Saunders' house."

"Okay. Stay by the phone."

I looked up. Mrs. Saunders stood in the doorway strangling a dish towel. Hope fluttered in her eyes despite all her denials. "Do you think it's the one who did it? Do you think you can find him?"

"I don't know. Let's see what Pete says." I went by her to the kitchen to get some more coffee and squeezed her wrist. She smiled, something I hadn't seen before. It was a nice smile.

Molasses minutes dripped by and hardened into a pool of the past. I had to take a leak, but was afraid to leave the phone. Renal failure backoned when it finally rang.

"Yes?"

"You were right, Haggerty. We used the reverse directories to get a name and address. I'm going out there now after we get a search warrant signed. Want to come along?"

"You bet."

"I'll pick you up in fifteen minutes. We're rousting a magistrate right now."

"Okay." I hung up. Maggie was still in the doorway, still doing murder with her hands.

"We may have a lead. Pete is coming by for me. Do you want to come too?"

She nodded her head. "Yes, yes I do."

"Let's get you a coat." I steered her to the closet, picked one out for her. She didn't dispute my choice, and I slipped it on her. If her hopes were doing their one hundred twenty-first performance as Lazarus, she was also retreating into herself. Keeping the ember alive and far from the wind. We went to the door and down to the street. I tossed the file in my car. In a few minutes DeVito pulled up. He rolled down his window. "Hello, Maggie. Are you sure you want to do this?"

"Yes, Pete. I'm sure. Let's go. Please."

I pulled open the door and we got in. DeVito turned to speak to us. "Guy's name is Justin Randolph. Lives over in Rockville. A complete forensics team is assembling over there. Everyone came, Maggie, everyone. I didn't have to ask twice."

"Thank you, Pete."

"This is how I want to do things Leo. It's an official police investigation. I've got my paperwork letter-perfect. We're going to do this one by the book. No loopholes. None. You understand?"

"Yeah. I stay outside until it's all over, and on the side you'll tell me anything I can use."

"You got it. Maggie, you too. Outside. As soon as we know anything, I'll tell you. I promise. You know that, right?"

"I know, Pete. Thank you."

Fifteen minutes later we pulled up to the house along with the lab truck and two other unmarked cars. As we all got out, DeVito grabbed my wrist. "Keep her out here, okay? God knows what we may find in there."

"I will, don't worry." DeVito nodded thanks and went to confer with his men. They were deployed around the house. I guided Mrs. Saunders back to the car.

DeVito unbuttoned his coat, pulled out his warrant, and began to approach the house.

I decided that standing out in the open under a streetlight

was pretty dumb so I moved Mrs. Saunders behind the lab truck. A firefight was not impossible.

DeVito was talking to someone at the door. Then he and his men disappeared inside. Maggie Saunders clutched at my coat sleeve. I felt pity for her dish rang. No sounds. The house had just absorbed the men. Then lights came on everywhere. Men were tromping up and down the stairs. DeVito came out and trotted back to us.

"He's not here, but Herb was. He said he was a computer salesman. The guy's on vacation. A little Carolina beach town near a ferry. We found a map in his study. He's in Bogue Beach. Here's his description from the cleaning woman.

"Why don't you do down there and try to find Herb. I'm going to try to get an okay from the chief to go down and look for Randolph, also get the paperwork going to get the Carolina cops looking for this guy. The lab guys are going to tear this place apart."

I looked at Maggie. "What do you say? I can fly down tonight. I don't have any paperwork to do or okays to get but yours. Don't worry about the cost. I still have twenty-four hours to try to earn my fee."

"Okay. Go ahead."

I had turned back to Pete when she said. "Can I go along?"

"I really don't think that would be wise. I know you want to be there, but frankly, this could get pretty wild down there. I'd function a lot better without worrying about you. I'll call as soon as I know anything. I promise." A litany of optimism everyone seemed to use around her.

She seemed to accept that, and I asked DeVito to drop us off back at her house so I could arrange a flight to North Carolina.

Chapter 11

At the house I decided not to go back in.

"Stay by the phone, Mrs. Saunders."

She squeezed my hands. She didn't want to let go. People had a habit of not coming back to her. "It's a small town. I'll find him." I didn't say anything about what would happen if he found Randolph first. She let go and trudged back to her house. I went off to mine.

I packed my bag quickly and called National Airport. There was only one flight a day down to Jacksonville, North Carolina, about an hour's drive away from Bogue Beach. It left each day at 3:30. Too long a wait. I could drive there in six hours or so. Worst case, I wouldn't get a motel room and I'd have to spend a night in my car. I threw together a bag of clothes, a shaving kit, a book, and some tools of the trade. Checked out a map, drew a route to the ocean, told my service I was going, locked up, and left. The Camaro was tanked up. I tossed in my bag, spread out the map, tucked it under the bag, and headed out into the night. ETA Bogue Beach: 2 A.M.

Three-and-a-half hours later I crossed the Carolina line, got off I-95 at Weldon, and started my back-roads trek. A sixty mile slant through Carolina farmland to the Ocean Highway through Halifax, Scotland Neck, Hamilton, to Williamston. I blew through the night at a steady seventy with pauses for the one light in each town. I had only the darkness for company. Around midnight I hit the Ocean Highway, a strangely named piece of road that never sees the sea. At a light I checked the map: Washington, Chocowinity, Vanceboro to New Bern. Another hour to Carolina 70. The light changed and I was gone. A one-man razorblade cutting along the dotted white line of caution. Moving smoothly through time and space, shearing through memory and desire.

All my life I'd used my cars as ambulances; Rescue from all my emotional emergencies. I rolled down the window. I could feel the wind through my hair, up my arm. Alone with that friction and the abrasive darkness, trying only to hold the line, I felt my cares being scrubbed away. I was a seventy-mile-an-hour bullet aimed right at the heart of eternity. For a dizzying moment I almost thought I'd get free. I wasn't even sure I knew what I was running from. But like all the times before it would be there in the morning when I arrived. Just another appointment in Samarra.

I re-entered at New Bern, got onto Carolina 70, and headed into the Croatan National Forest. Eight years ago, somewhere in those woods, somebody set fire to the bodies of Bradford Bishops' mother, wife, and three kids. A lot of cops think old Bradford did it. They sure want to ask him about it. When he disappeared into the Great Smoky Mountains, he left the pages of history and became one of Washington, D.C.'s legends.

Around two I pulled into the outskirts of Morehead City and started to look for motels. Morehead's a small town of about 4,000 souls on the way to Bogue Beach. Everything was dark. I went down Main Street until I saw the sign for the beach towns. Turning right I figured I'd give Bogue Beach itself a try. If worst came to worst, park on a side street and get some shut-eye in the car. Only the darkness awaited me.

I pulled up to the main intersection in town, nothing down either side road. Straight ahead, opposite the gas station, some lights were on. I pulled around to the far side. It wasn't a motel, but a bar: The Rebel Yell. Funny that it was still lit. All the others were dark. The owner probably forgot to hit the lights on the way out. Too bad. I could really use a bathroom. As I rolled by it, a guy came out of the bar and hurried out to the lone car in the parking lot. He had the whitewalls of a Marine.

I remembered that LeJeune was nearby. Since Lebanon and Grenada, they'd be all over this town on leave like they were on standby for the ark. The guy fumbled with a ring of keys for the door. He was probably so fucked up he shouldn't be driving, but at this time of night he'd most likely just kill himself. I pulled up alongside him. The car had California tags and a UC-Berkeley sticker. Probably family visiting. I slid out of the car, stretched and walked up to the bar door. The guy was startled to see me. He looked away immediately and kept fumbling with the keys. I checked to see if I had forgotten my pants or something, and pulled at the door. It felt stuck so I pulled harder. It popped open and I was facing another man. His eyes were open wide, also surprised to see me. Like I was the Easter Bunny and damned early. He let go of the door, and I slid past him. There were four good old boys with their boots up on the table sucking at beers. Another one was staring at the jukebox looking no brighter than the RCA dog. Lynyrd Skynyrd poured out of the box. The bartender had company: another country boy, shirt sleeves rolled up showing a tattoo of the Marine insignia or a serpent crawling around some other damned foolishness. He had his hands on the old man's forearm. He wouldn't look at me. Everything was freeze frame with high resolution paranoia. My chest was starting to knit cross hairs. These boys had firing-squad eyes.

"Boy, I'm glad you're still open. My bladder was ready to bust." I unbuttoned my jacket and cricked my back like I had kidney pains. My shit-eating grin hadn't defused anyone. If this was a clandestine meeting I could give a shit. I saw the bathroom signs and made for them.

One of the boys kicked back his chair, "Hey, man, we're—"

Then the guy behind the bar spoke up. "Watchya want?"

"I just want to take a leak and I'm gone." I kept moving to the back.

"Men's room's broken. Sorry." He smiled and put both his hands on the bar.

"All right. I'll use the ladies' head. I ain't particular."

"All right. Hurry up. We gotta close."

He started to say something else, and I was around the corner. In the dark a cigarette glowed. Another one, with his leg extended across the hallway. He pointed to my right. I saw "Ladies" on the door, smiled at him, put my hands up, and backed into it. I unzipped my fly and took a leak. Shit. Something smelled rotten a long way from Denmark. A dope deal? Who gave a fuck? Not me. I searched the wall with my eyes. No openings. Bars on the window to the outside. I went to the sink to wash my hands. The bathroom was clean. Probably a lot better than the men's room would have been. I'll have to thank them on the way out.

There was a thump against the wall, then another. I squatted down and saw a small gap in the wall around the sink pipes. I put my face up against it. There was a face on the floor. The one eye I could see was purple and closed. There was a trickle of blood from the corner of the mouth. Fuck. I go into a bar to take a leak and find a stiff. Be cool. I'm leaving while I can.

The eye opened. Wide. There was another dull thump. A wince. Shit, it's alive. Worse yet. I stood up and ran the water for no reason at all. I took a deep breath and got none. The gentle hand of fear was on me. I looked around. Time for a Riggo drill. Coming straight at you. A hog, a hog. My kingdom for a hog. I pushed back my jacket and drew out my .45. The sieve of judgment was growing finer all the time. Once drawn you'd best be ready to use it. I pulled open the door with my arm behind me.

"You got a light?"

"Yeah." The guy in the hall reached into his pants pocket, and I pistol-whipped him right there. His head snapped back like a Dutch door. First down and goal. He sagged into my arms. I put Dutch in front of me as a shield, cocked my gun, and gently pushed the men's room door open. A man on his knees was thrusting and grunting into a very unwilling woman. Her head thumped against the sink stand. The woman looked barely conscious. I dropped Dutch, slid up behind Thumper, and grabbed him. "Make a sound and I'll pull them off like grapes."

He nodded. A quick study.

"Party's over, sport. We're leaving now."

Another nod.

"Listen good. You give me any trouble going out of here and your buddies are gonna have your brains in their beer. Got it? Good."

"You the heat?"

"Don't worry about the heat, sport. As far as you're concerned, I'm the fire itself."

He moved away at my gentle tug and stayed on all fours. I shook the girl. One eye opened. She pushed over on to her side. Curled up with her bruised belly, she looked like a battered fetus. The other eye was closed, her nose caked with blood. One earlobe was torn. She reached up to her face, opened her mouth, and pulled out her wadded up underpants. I pushed the gun against Thumper's head and almost killed him. Instead, I rapped him across the collarbone. It broke like a dry twig. The girl had pulled her legs up in front of her and was scuttling away from me. Her eyes were looking for her clothes.

I shucked off my coat. "I'm sorry, but we ain't got time for you to get dressed. Put this on. We've gotta go now." Her back was still to me. Company had to be coming soon. Nobody took this long to piss.

"Do you hear me?" Nothing

I looked square at Thumper, "Sit." I reached down and got an arm around the girl's waist and pulled her up to her feet. She groaned as I pressed on her ribs. She was dead weight.

"Put an arm around my neck. I'll carry you out of here. Let's go." I waved my gun at the guy. He wavered. "Walk or die."

Naked, he got up and went out the door in front of me. We'd just made it. No delay of game. Two of the residents were in the doorway to the hall. I fired once over their heads. Barely. They backed off. I maneuvered out into the room with my companions. "Into the corner everyone. Hands high."

The one behind the bar barked, "Jesus, man. What're you doin'? That whore made a deal . . ."

I put a hole in the wall behind him. "Shove it."

I counted heads. All present and accounted for. We backed up toward the door. I turned the knob. It was locked. "Not smart, not smart at all. Guess I wasn't expected to leave, huh?" I got flat glassy stares. I pointed the gun at the one on the left. "Okay. We'll start with you. You want to die for a door key?"

He flinched and looked back at the bar. "Jesus, Beau, give him the key already."

Beau went for his pants pocket. "Easy, Beau. Go slow or die fast."

He came up with the key, looked sadly at it, and tossed it to me. It hit me in the chest. I waved at Thumper. "Pick it up and put it in the door. Now."

He bent down, all pale white and goosefleshy, picked up the key, and unlocked the door. I pointed the gun at his head. "Back out slow with me." As we went through the door I looked straight at Beau. "First one through the door gets a .45 caliber forget-me-not."

I hobbled with the girl over to the car, draped her across

the hood, pulled out my keys, opened the trunk, and motioned for the guy to climb in.

"Ah, Jesus. Not in there, I'll die. I mean I can't take it. Anything else. Don't lock me up in there."

"Shut up, asshole, and get in. I'm losing my sunny disposition all of a sudden."

He slowly climbed in and huddled up. I slammed the lid on him. Christ. I went around the car and opened my door and pushed the girl across the seat. She went in like a sack. I climbed in and kept my eye on the bar door. The Camaro turned over, and we backed away from the bar. I headed back down the road toward the center of town.

The road was straight and narrow. Sea oats moved in the breeze on the windward side. The roll of the breakers beyond the dunes gave me no peace at all. I looked over at my traveling companion swathed in my coat. She was curled up away from me, her head on the door frame.

"Can you hear me? I'm taking you to the police station and then we'll get you to a doctor, get you looked at." Nothing. "You hear me? It's all over. All over." Nothing. All over, my ass. This was syndicated rerun time now playing in the theatre of your mind.

Chapter 12

We came upon a blue sign that read Coastal Emergency Clinic. I pulled into the entrance road. She'd get taken care of first. Country boy could wait. I pulled up to the sliding glass doors, killed the car, hopped out, ran through the overhead eye beam. A nurse on duty behind the desk looked up, said quizzically, "Yes?"

"I've got a girl in my car. She's been raped. Head injuries and abdominal injuries."

She pushed an intercom button. "Dr. Lefcort, this is Lee. We have an admission. Rape with head injuries."

"On my way."

I looked back at the car and saw a tall stoop-shouldered hippy man with a laurel wreath of graying hair heading that way. I walked out to the car and opened the door. As I stepped back, he slid in next to the girl.

"Young lady, my name is Dr. Lefcort. Can you hear me? If you can, please say so. If you cannot speak, nod."

Her eyes were still welded shut, but she spoke very softly, "I hear you."

"Very good. I'm going to ask you to do some things before we try to move you. Okay?" She nodded to that.

"Move your toes. Wiggle them." We looked down. "Very good. Now I'm going to put out my hands, please take them in your hands and squeeze them as hard as you can. Will you do that?" She was still huddled up. I looked back at the gurney that was now behind Lefcort, took a gown off it, and draped it over her.

"Try now, okay?"

She looked up at me for an instant and fixed me with eyes one shade too blue. I saw a broad high forehead tapering past cheekbones that would cut paper to a once thin-lipped mouth and faintly cleft chin. She had short black hair parted high, one wing swept back over her ear the other hung insolently over one eye. Her skin, where it wasn't purple yellow, was skim milk white and her nose, once aquiline, was swelling like bread. She unhugged herself and squeezed Lefcort's hand. "Good, Okay. I'm going to touch you with a stethoscope to check your lungs and then take your pulse. Okay?" He warmed up the stethoscope and checked her breathing. "Good, good. Lungs sound okay." He held her pulse and counted silently to himself.

He looked up at me. "Mr. — ?"

"Haggerty."

"And I will help you up onto the gurney and get you in for an examination. Ready?" She nodded yes.

I squatted and got a hand on her thighs and back and lifted her up with Lefcort. She was big, probably a hundred-and-fifty pounds. I'd backed out of the bar with her hanging from my neck like an amulet and hadn't felt a thing. Love that adrenaline. Lefcort slid the gurney over and stepped back. I hoisted her up over the edge and let her slowly unclench herself. I pulled my hand out from beneath her and patted her arm. She looked up at me and tried to say something. I bent down to her.

"Thank you."

I just patted her arm, suddenly stupid. Once she laid her head back, Dr. Lefcort put sandbags on either side of her head. "Don't worry. These are only to keep your head still. I want some pictures of your neck and face when we get you inside." He wheeled her into an examining room and began snapping off commands. "All right, let's get moving. I want skull and chest pictures." He turned to me.

"Are you family?"

"No."

"Okay. I'm sorry. I appreciate your help here, but unless you're family you'll have to leave."

I felt the girl's fingers grip for and squeeze my hand.

"I really don't think she should be alone right now, Doctor. And even if I'm not family, she's a client of mine and I do have certain obligations to her and her family."

"Client? What kind of client, Mr. Haggerty?"

"I'm a private detective. Hired by Miss — ?"

I sent her a telepathic command.

"Sullivan. Wendy Sullivan," she said.

Atta girl. She moved her puffy lips around the words like they were wooden blocks she'd eaten.

"First, we need a little information from you, Ms. Sullivan."

After getting her address and phone number, he went on to her parents' names.

"Peter and Janet Sullivan."

"Address."

"Same."

"Birthdate."

"March 31, 1964."

" Do you have a local address, Miss Sullivan?"

"Yes. 515 Oceanside Lane."

"Phone."

"I don't know it. My folks are just renting it for the year. My father's here on sabbatical. I came ahead to open up for them."

"Can we call them in San Francisco?"

"No. They're starting up from Florida. He was there on a lecture tour. They should be here Friday or Saturday."

"What does your father do?"

"He's a marine biologist here to do research at the University Marine Labs."

"Oh. Is there anyone else we can call?"

"No. There's no one else."

"All right. I'm going to get X-rays of your chest and face, and do a general exam for other injuries."

Wendy nodded. Dr. Lefcort rechecked her pulse and took her blood pressure. He gently pushed on her abdomen looking for injury beyond the bruises and looked at her teeth, nose, and face.

"Okay, we're going to wheel you down to X-ray."

I left Dr. Lefcort and went up to the admitting desk. "Have you called the police?"

"Yes. I did right away. I'm sure they'll be here very soon."

I turned back and stared into the darkness. Inside I was just as formless as the night. With a simpleton's persistence, I stroked my mustache. A blue light flashed across my field of vision. I heard the gurney's wheels clacking on the linoleum floor and turned back to Wendy.

Dr. Lefcort wheeled her into the examining room and said, "I would like to examine you and treat you for the injuries you've suffered. Evidence obtained in this examination may be used in court if you decide to proceed with charges. There is no need to decide now, but we would like you to consent to allow us to collect such evidence now in case you do later decide to report it." Lefcort looked as uncomfortable as his speech had been awkward.

"Okay. I want to press charges. What do we have to do?"

"First I want to photograph your injuries. Then I'll need to put your clothes in a bag for the police. By the way, where are your clothes? I didn't notice any."

I spoke up. "We left them behind. I didn't think we had time to gather them up and get out."

"Okay. We'll need a combing of your pubic hair, and we'll

have to do a pelvic exam and take smears, depending on, you know, what kind of things happened." Lefcort's detachment was disapparing, and his soft white hands fluttered like doves trying to flee his wrists.

"Anyway, we'll treat and test you for venereal disease and the possibility of pregnancy. You'll need to follow up with retests in two weeks."

There was a knock on the door, and then a hand reached in with the X-rays. Lefcort clipped them up, lit them, and peered closely at them. "Very good, good. your ribs aren't broken, and the zygoma—that's your cheekbone—is not fractured. Your teeth are okay—no broken roots under the gums—and your nose isn't broken. The swelling is from the upper lip. We'll suture up that earlobe. How did that happen?"

"One of them bit me."

"Oh." Lefcort was sorry he asked.

"Would you like privacy for this exam, Miss Sullivan?"

"Yes, Please."

"Um, I'll be right outside if you want me, okay?"

I walked out and leaned against the wall for a while. Then I did my caged tiger routine. Lazy figure eights up and down the hall. I'd rather bleed than wait.

The examining room door was pulled open. Lefcort stepped out and waved to me.

"Would you please come in, Mr. Haggerty. We were going to do the pelvic, and she began crying and froze up. Perhaps you could help calm her down."

"Sure."

She was on her side turned away from us. Curled up and crying, not the totality of sobbing, but still a full deep cry.

"Wendy, this is Leo Haggerty. Take my hand. Listen. I know this is real hard to do. I bet it feels just like it's happening all over again. Nobody's going to hurt you here. Just look at me. Come on. Roll over. That's the way to go. Now look at my face. Try to concentrate on it and relax. Breathe as deeply as you can and relax. The doctor'll be done in no time. Focus on me. What do you see? I'm a beauty, ain't I?"

"Yeah."

"Movie star features, right?"

"Sure."

"I mean, are these Newman's eyes or what?"

"No."

"Is this Jack Nicholson's smile?"

"No."

"Okay. It's his hairline for sure."

She smiled for only the briefest instant. I was losing her. I took a different tack.

"You live in Berkeley. Go to school there?"

"Uh huh."

"What're you studying?"

"Just liberal arts. I'm a sophomore. I haven't decided."

"Berkeley's a beautiful place. I've got friends who live out there. The view at night is something else, isn't it?"

"Yeah."

"You know the merry-go-round up in Tilden Park?"

"Yeah. I used to ride it when I was a kid."

"Okay, Miss Sullivan, we're done. We're going to take blood and urine samples and give you some penicillin. You're not allergic are you?"

"No."

A nurse poked her head in. "Mr. Haggerty, there's a police officer here." I patted the girl's arm.

"Listen, I'll be right outside if you need me."

I went through the door, and the cop was right in front of me. He reached up and yanked my gun from its holster. His other hand was already coming up. It was full.

"Freeze."

I froze and grew a knot in my throat like I'd eaten a moose, antlers and all. "What the hell's going on here?"

"Shut up. I'm asking the questions. Turn around and put your hands on the wall."

He spun me around and rammed his gun into my kidneys and frisked me.

"Listen, I placed the call and reported the rape."

"What rape? I got you on armed kidnapping, carrying a concealed weapon, assault and battery, filing a false report." He pulled my hands down behind me and cuffed me numbingly tight. My hands would be dead in two minutes. This is usually the prelude to a session of pound the penguin. It's an indoor sport, so named because the man with the dead arms who can't lift them to defend himself or keep himself upright, who waddles around and bumps into walls, looks like a penguin trying to fly. The object is to hit the penguin until it can't get up any more. Then the game's over. First your hands are dead. Then a couple of shots with a night stick on the elbow and shoulder and your arms are dead too. Then they take off the cuffs. By then, you couldn't fend off a girl scout. So they get all the freebies they want. You hope you don't take too many to the head and the boys get arm weary or decide watching you barf is less interesting than playing Pac Man.

I remembered my last session as a penguin. Panic's icy slush filled my veins.

He spun me around and said, "DuWayne, this the guy kidnapped you?" The occupant of my trunk was standing next to him. The cop must have heard him pounding on it when he got here and let him out. DuWayne was wearing a hospital gown.

"Yeah. He's the one. The bitch must be here somewhere too."

"All right. DuWayne, you get your shoulder fixed up and come on down to the station to fill out the complaint." He turned back to him and stared at him. "Right away. Do you

understand?" The last instruction was burdened with over-
tones. DuWayne skulked away. DuWayne. Jesus, what a
name. It sounded like a guitar string snapping. He turned
back to me.

"All right, where's the whore?"

"I don't know what you're talking about. You want to bury
me, you're gonna have to earn it, sport. I ain't gonna give
it to you on a platter." I stared at the cop. Wiry little fuck.
Ropy muscles. Hard flat planes to his face. Live wire eyes
and the smile of a junkyard dog.

The door behind me opened, and Dr. Lefcort came out.
"Miss Sullivan is ready to . . ." His eyes opened wider and
his voice left through them. The cop pushed me through the
door. Wendy was sitting on the edge of the bed, dressed in
some odds and ends they must have had on hand.

"Don't move. You're under arrest." Wendy stared at me.

"Don't say anything. We'll get a call to our lawyers. It's
a frame."

"Shut up, smart ass. That call could be a long time coming." He looked to see if Lefcort had followed us and then
grabbed me by the cuffs and yanked my arms up. I sang in
an unfamiliar register.

"What am I being arrested for? I was raped." Wendy's voice
began to break. We were crossing the nightmare county line.

"What rape? I got six witnesses say you solicited them for
sex for money and everything was fine until this guy busted
in and kidnapped one of the guys. So I got you on solicitation."

"What? Look at me." She had bandages on her ear, nose,
and cheek and bruises for garnish.

"So you like it rough. Let's go. I ain't gonna argue with
you. You're under arrest. I don't want to cuff you if I don't
have to, but don't push it." He grabbed her arm by the elbow
and steered us both out through the lobby. I saw Lefcort
staring at us.

"Call the FBI. They're going to kill us. It's a cover-up for the guys who—"

One well-concealed yank and my brain lit up like a Pentagon war board. We were out and into the squad car. Me in the back, Wendy up front. I couldn't hear what he was saying to her, but her face went from hopeful misunderstanding to anger then fear, through revulsion and stopped at numbed defeat.

We pulled up at the station. The cop led Wendy inside and left me to ripen. After a few minutes he returned and pulled me out of the car. Standing next to me in the dark, not looking at me, he began to talk. He spoke softly as if coaxing a wary bird out of the brush.

"Let's talk. I made my offer to the girl: Forget about tonight or stand trial and take her chances. It'll be pretty ugly for her, but you know that. Allegations about being a whore. Descriptions of what she liked best with each guy. You know the scene. This is church country. What's this girl doing out alone at night in a bar? She must a been looking for trouble. She's from California. They're all crazy out there anyway, not decent folk.

"Now you, you're looking at a lot of time. Felony with a firearm, that's a sure seven for starters. No short time on that. Now I'll admit she's a fine piece of tail. Lot of woman there, but what do you care for? You don't know her; she's a stranger to you. Do you really want to take the chance of hard time for a stranger? Suppose we make the solicitation stick. The rape goes out the window, and you take the fall. She does sixty days at the county farm. The guys in the bar go back to drinking and telling tales about this jerk who passed through and made one hell of a big mistake, and you're sittin' in the pen up at Tillery doing seven for starters, maybe another fifteen. You know what happens to a white boy up there. You'd have an asshole you could park a combine in." He shook out a cigarette, tamped it down, lit up, exhaled, and went on.

"I want you to know there ain't no hard feelings with you. We can keep DuWayne quiet. He's a jerk anyway. They understand you doin' what you did. Even respect it. It took balls to back them all down, but they ain't about to just roll over and take a fall for this. I mean, you agree to play ball, the girl forgets about it, everybody walks away happy. No hard feelings. If not, and they don't fuck you cross-eyed at Tillery — and maybe they wouldn't, you're a pretty hard dude. You kick a few asses, hook up with the Aryan brotherhood, you make your time, and you can still fart. Do you really want to do twenty years worrying about catchin' a shank? Hell, you get out, you're an old man. No young girls for you. Your life's over. For what? I ask you. For what? She your daughter? You gonna marry her? Think about it."

He took me by the elbow and guided me to the station. I was thinking about it, hard. Real hard. He smiled that junk-yard dog's grin, "But don't take too long now, you hear?"

"I hear."

This was one small station. He was the only cop pulling night shift. Up front I could hear the crackle of the dispatcher's microphone and see her blueclad backside. She hadn't seen us come in the prisoner's entrance.

We went in. I was booked. My personal property was tagged and bagged. My P.I. license got me a second look, but that was it. My gun was taken as evidence. Everything was smooth and regulation except no offer of a phone call and no Miranda. I took a last look at my watch. I guess he'd asked the only question he cared about. The cop took me back to one of the cells. Wendy was in the one next to me. Dogface said, "Maybe you two want to talk. We're supposed to segregate the men and the women, but this is a small town. Don't hardly ever have two people in here at the same time. Don't get any cute ideas on making a ruckus back here. It won't do you no good. Along with the kidnapping and solicitation, you're on paper as disorderly in public, resisting arrest, and possession with intent to distribute a controlled substance. Of course a further investigation might yield additional charges, but right now you're at least a couple of paranoid dopers yelling 'police brutality,' and ain't nobody gonna listen to you. You run your mouths and I'll have you gagged and straitjacketed. I'll be out front if you want me."

We ignored him. I figured this was what the Burger Court would call a "good faith error" by the police and I was just being a poor sport about it.

"You okay?"

"No. I'm not okay."

"I mean he didn't hurt you or anything did he?"

"No. He just made it clear what would happen if I pressed charges."

"What are you going to do?"

"I don't know. I'm scared. I mean really scared. But I get sick when I think of just letting them get away with what they did. What'd he say to you?"

"He told me I was a fool to risk a long prison sentence for a stranger. He also gave me a refresher course on the pleasures of prison life before I came out an old man."

"Do you think you're a fool?"

Those damn blue eyes again and that insolent wing of jet black hair. "No. Don't get me wrong, now. I'm not happy about this. I don't get off risking my life. I want to die old, fat, and happy. I won't stay behind making a fuss if you decide to walk away from it. If you want to fight it then I'll fight it with you, as simple as that. I wouldn't leave you here in this jail any more than I would've walked away from you in that bar."

"Can we beat them? Can they make it stick?"

"I don't know how tight the frame is. Dogface is just a bent cop, but if the chief's his cousin and the county judge is his uncle, they could bury us here and no one would ever know.

I've got a damn good lawyer who'd turn this county inside out to get me out, once he knew I was here. There's a cop from Maryland who knows I'm here. He'd start to look after a while. Your folks will start looking for you when they arrive. I don't think they'd kill us to keep this covered up, but depending on who's willing to break the rules, we could both go to jail. The law's just a recipe that if you follow, most of the time you get justice. But they've made it real clear that they'll fuck around with the ingredients. We could get the shaft."

"Why do this to us?"

"Money, perhaps. Dogface could have been paid a ton to bring us in. It would have to be a lot for him to risk this, unless the whole town is crooked, because he could go to jail and cops don't thrive in prison. Or it's personal. He's covering up for somebody — a cousin, a brother. We don't know who the men in there were. If it's personal then we're in better shape because the frame probably won't extend beyond him unless — "

"The chief's his uncle, etc. etc."

"You've got it. If there's a decent cop anywhere in this town, I think we can make the charge stick. But that's a big if. I'm sorry I can't give you a better idea on what to do."

She looked at me. For the first time I appreciated her presence. She had to be as tall as I was. Six feet, broad shouldered, slim hipped, long legged. She wrapped her hands around the bars and rocked back and forth on her heels. She looked back at me. Big bright eyes lit up the expanse of her forehead. Below, the razor edge cheekbones, patrician nose, and thin lips would keep secrets well. Her eyes would say what her lips never could. "Isn't this where one of us turns into the Incredible Hulk and gets us out of here?"

"Don't let me stop you."

She slid her hands through the bars. "I'm sorry you're in this. I just can't take that on for you. He said if I was convicted

I'd only go to some county farm. I could risk that or being embarrassed down here, who cares. But I couldn't take the chance of your going to prison for twenty years. Let's just drop it and get out of here." She banged her palm against the bars. "Damn! I'd like to kill them. Damn."

"I'm really sorry. Sometimes the bad guys win, and this looks like one of those times, and it really shits."

We waited for dogface to return. Jail time began; that amorphous muddy river of eternity drifting by without discernible current. You're just there. Moving slower than you wish and stretching further than you can fear. That's the first thing you lose in jail: time, manageable time. Slowly jail time coalesces around the daily rituals. The day and night cycles are reinvented. Like brackets or parentheses, you get activated to eat and exercise or work. Then you wait, knowing it won't be forever and that a day is a day. We'd dropped out of time into limbo awaiting dogface's whim. I figured we'd been here about a half an hour and I'd been booked at about 4:15. The day shift would come on about 8. I'd take my chances with his paranoid doper bullshit. If that flew they were training cops in seminaries these days. If this was as small a town as I thought, the day shift would notice us. At least Wendy would attract attention. We'd know by then if this was dogface's scam or a regular township project.

"Let's wait him out. If he's not alone in this a few hours won't hurt. But if he's trying this all on his own, the longer we wait the harder it will be for him to pull it off."

Wendy nodded and walked off to her cot and folded herself up on it, back against the wall. I don't wait worth a shit and would've talked her ear off, but she didn't seem to want to. The minutes dripped on like sweat off the end of your nose. Each one getting bigger and fatter 'til it can't do anything but move on. I paced, counted bars, tiles, read graffiti, sat, stood, walked, leaned, and finally slept.

Chapter 13

MY DREAMS WERE BAD, BUT BRIEF. I'D NEVER LEARNED TO RELAX in captivity, and didn't especially want to, so the first faint footfalls woke me. Two men in uniforms had their backs to me looking in Wendy's cell. The uniforms were different than what I'd remembered of Dogface's. State cops? Sheriffs? This was my chance. I rolled off my concrete bunk and came up behind the two cops. "Hey. Help us." My voice startled them. They straightened up and turned toward me. "We're being held . . ." They were smiling. Oh shit. It was Dutch and the RCA Dog from the bar. I was starting to feel like a Jew on opening day at Belsen. You have to do one full lap around hell before you can begin to plot your escape. You need to know its true dimensions. Right now the course was getting longer and there was no end in sight.

"Well, well. The Lone Ranger," Dutch drawled. "No matter what happens here, I'm gonna get you for what you did to me, motherfucker. Believe it."

I just stood there and let him run his mouth. I was in no position to aggravate anyone. I silently confirmed that their uniforms were different from Dogface's. Their shoulder patches said they were in the reserves. That made sense. In high season on a weekend this town might swell up thirty to forty times its normal size. Engorged with vacationers, they'd need an auxiliary force just to handle the traffic. My last wisps of hope blew down the corridor.

They turned back to Wendy. The other guy pulled something out of his pocket, snaked his arm through the bars, and threw it at her. It hit her in the forehead, and her eyes popped open. "Hey missy, you lonely in there? Want some company? We ain't done with you yet, sweetpea, not by a long shot. Sure hope you got your energy back, sugar."

His laugh stiffened my spine like a spider's feathery touch. I was right up against the bars, all eyes. My darkest hopes and wishes coiled behind my lids like a cobra in its basket. I remembered an alligator I knew in Florida. Every year I'd go visit him. Unmoving, day after day he'd just lie there in the sun, staring at the people who came to look at him, who threw pennies on his snout. I swear I never saw him move. Then one day, in a flash he just rose up and tore off a woman's arm. I just hoped my day would come.

The prisoner entrance clicked open and wooshed shut. We all turned toward the sound. Dogface came in and pulled up short, obviously surprised to see the two men in the hall. "What the hell are you doin' here?"

"We just thought we'd come by and refresh her memory 'bout what might happen to her, Elroy."

"You idiots. I told you I'd handle it. Goddammit. Who's idea was this? Bubba's? You want to blow this all to hell? I got it fixed good. Just let me do it my way. I told Beau I'd handle it. Get the fuck outta here. You're screwing everything up."

"Excuse me, Elroy, but I've been looking over the incident cards and . . ." The dispatcher had come back from her desk. Her eyes took everyone in. Wide-eyed Wendy, angry Elroy, the two rapist reservists, and me. Her voice and her smile took the tiniest dips during that once-over, but she was perky at the finish. "I just need you to sign off on them, uh, whenever you can." She waved to no one in particular and only I, from the corner of my cell, saw her face fall, settle, and then compose itself. Like a crash landing you walk away from. The door banged behind her.

Elroy turned back to the two men. "Get out of here. There can't be any connection between DuWayne or Beau and me. I fixed it like that, and now you're messing it up. Let me do this my way. Get out of here."

The two guys looked at each other for permission to leave and once granted, scuttled hurriedly out the back door. Elroy looked real unhappy. He turned around once in the hallway, looking at Wendy and then me like unexpected in-laws on his doorstep. He mopped his brow, realigned his hat, and went up to see what the dispatcher wanted.

I looked over at Wendy. "Hot damn. I think someone just slammed the door on Elroy's soufflé."

She didn't smile back or look even remotely reassured. The message these men delivered had gone all the way through her. She was sinking and I was rearranging the deck chairs.

A few hours later Elroy returned. He rattled the bars with his nightstick. "Get up, dammit." I looked up at him trying to read him. "Look, I tried to reason with you, do this the easy way. You ain't givin' me no choice. You play hardball and you'll find yourself so far up shit's creek the sun won't find you. I mean it. Even if you get bail. How long you think you'll last out there? You can't leave town and this ain't your town, it's theirs. You could have an accident, both of you. A bad accident." Dogface was real upset. Maybe it was turning to shit on him. Or was this just another threat. I had the feeling the frame wasn't going to stick. Maybe the day shift was in, and he couldn't keep this hidden much longer.

The door opened up to the cell block, and we had company. Company was short and squat, encased in a too tight blue seersucker suit. He had no hair and no neck. Piggy eyes, an upturned snout, and a nasty cupid's mouth. This wasn't Porky Pig. This was a wild boar. He had a sheaf of papers in his hand. He smiled at Elroy and rolled over to him. "Hello Elroy, thought I'd stop by 'fore I leave town for that chief's meeting. What we got here, Elroy?" He was all twinkly eyed and simper smiley.

"Well, Chief . . ."

"Well what, Elroy? I've got a report here says we've got an armed kidnapper and a psychotic masochistic whore over there. Goddam, Elroy. I've been a cop fourteen years, ain't never seen a case like this. Tell me about it. I admire good police work. You know that." Porky was beginning to resemble a blood sausage.

"Well, I got this call."

"Yeah, I read about that. You went out and interviewed all of the 'witnesses' at once. Took a composite statement. Hell, that's efficient. Saves paper. Makes for good reading. Elroy, what is this I'm reading? You got seven cretins out there couldn't agree on Jesus Christ's first name and here they are singin' sweet harmony like the Mormon Tabernacle Choir. Hell of a job. Hell of a job." Leading with his chin and belly, the chief was herding Elroy back toward the corner of the cell block.

He waved the papers at Wendy. "Tell me about her, Elroy. Ain't she the strangest woman you ever met? Regular Kookifornian, right? Tell me about her, Elroy. I'm interested in abnormal psychology. You know I preach the importance of motivation. I'm waiting."

Elroy was a whipped dogface. Eyes down, shoulders hunched, looking for a way to escape. Elroy squeaked, "There was four hundred dollars in her wallet and her clothes were all neatly folded up when I got there."

Nice try. They took the night's receipts to make it look like she got paid.

"Jesus, Elroy. She was driving a BMW. It's not stolen. It's her father's car. She's driving a fifteen thousand dollar car and takes on a bar full of guys for four hundred bucks? She don't need money. Why'd she do it? For kicks? For no reason she pulls over to a road house walks in and offers to pull a train? She must be crazy. A fuckin' looney tune.

"Let me tell you about her. Elsie did her homework. Ran a PIN check on her after you booked her. Nothing Elroy. Nothing. Not even a traffic arrest. No DWIs, no priors for soliciting. What happened, Elroy? She just go batshit when she got to town? For no reason she thinks she's Penn Station? Goddammit." He shook his head. "Look at those injuries. That ain't rough sex, that's a beating. Rough sex you get torn nipples, bruised butts. Not broken noses. Christ, Elroy, what for? Your whole life's down the toidy. For what?"

Elroy couldn't face him.

"He's a shit, Elroy. A fucking animal. If you'd done your job she'd a gotten over it. Now you're both fucked. Who's gonna take care of her now? Jesus man, did you fuckin' blow it."

The chief put his hand on Elroy's shoulder and like a snake disarmed him with the other. "Gimme your badge, Elroy."

He took it and fished out the keys and opened my cell. "Come on out. I'm very sorry, Mr. Haggerty, about all this."

I passed Elroy in the doorway. Vestibule for the elevator of destiny. Going up?

The chief opened Wendy's cell. "Miss Sullivan, I'm Chief Maxwell Hungerford, and I apologize to you for everything you've been put through. Please believe me this is not how my department is run, and we will do everything in our power to apprehend and help convict the men who assaulted you." He held out his hand to help her over an invisible threshold. Hungerford showed us out of the cell block and asked us to sit in his office.

"Your cars are out of impoundment, and I'd like you to make sure all your property is accounted for. I've filed a 'bad arrest' report and all the records have been expunged. I want you to be assured that your records are clean."

"Thank you," we echoed.

"How'd you get involved, Chief Hungerford? I thought we were up the river."

"Dumb luck. This is a small town. There's less than 1,000 people here. I'm chief, and I've got three shifts with a dispatcher in the station and one or two officers on the road. Any emergencies come up, dispatcher calls me.

"Elroy got a personal call to him at the station. It must have been from the bar. He left to respond to it. Then your complaint came in. Elsie called Elroy. That's when he showed up at the clinic. But everything was ass-backward. If he was arresting you all, where was the complaint? The only call to the station was the personal one to Elroy. If you've got an armed kidnapping, why not call the police? Let us coordinate with Morehead and the state troopers. It smelled to Elsie, so she called me. Even if he took DuWayne's word over yours at the scene, the time it took to respond to a rape call was too damn long. That bothered Elsie. Elroy must a been working out the details at the bar. Then when Elsie wanted him to sign the incident card and she saw two of the guys on the complaint standing outside the cells, it smelled worse. It ain't a holiday weekend approaching. The reserves wouldn't be on duty. So she punched Miss Sullivan and the car on the computer. When everything came up squeaky clean she gave me a call.

"It smelled to me too, so I started doing some checking. If Elsie hadn't called me, I was leaving for a three day police chief's meeting in Charlotte with Elroy left in charge. He'd have had that long to try to get his cover-up in place."

"What was that you were saying to Elroy? It sounded like you knew why he did it."

"Yeah. I could figure it out. Beau Lundeen's his brother-in-law. Elroy's sister's mildly retarded. She's also pretty good lookin', and frankly, she put out pretty easy. That's why Lundeen married her. Elroy's always looked after her. He probably figured it'd break her heart if that shit she married got sent away. She loves that bastard no matter what he does. She can't see him for what he is. I guess he was tryin' to protect her, 'cause he's got no use for Lundeen. Damn fool just threw his whole life away. Hey, it's sad about his sister, don't misunderstand me. But you start running when you oughtta stand still, you wind up runnin' smack dab into something worse, and a cop in prison is about as bad as you can get. Brenda's gonna shed plenty of tears when this is all over.

"Look, this is my problem to deal with, not yours. I just want to apologize for this and let you know this office will prosecute those men responsible to the fullest extent of the law. I've got my other two officers out rounding them up right now. As I said, the arrest and all records pertaining to them will be completely expunged. Your records will both be clean. We'll return all your property to you, except, of course, your gun, Mr Haggerty. You can claim that when you leave town."

"Why?"

"Come on now. You've got no license to carry that thing here. The way things have been going anything can happen with that gun. I'd look like a damn fool giving it back to you. You already showed you aren't reluctant to use it."

"You expect I'm going to have a reason to?"

"No, not really. Those seven are pack animals. Not enough gumption among them to jaywalk alone. I'll try like hell to keep'em detained, but Judge McCandless' got a mind of his own. They're all working men with families, kids. He might grant them bail. They've got records, but nothing of this magnitude. He might let them loose, but I don't think you've got anything to fear. I'll keep my eyes open. If they get released I'll let them know that if either of you even gets a sunburn on the beach I'm gonna be all over them like flies at a picnic. But I'm down one man and those two 'reservists.' I've been trying to get those bastards off the force since I took over.

This isn't the way I wanted to do it though. I can't put you under surveillance. Where are you staying? I'll be sure we sweep there regularly."

"I haven't gotten a place yet. I'll let you know when I do."

"And you, miss?"

Wendy gave him her address.

"Oh yeah, on the ocean down near the state beach. Fine. After you've settled in, call me and arrange to come in and give us your statements."

Hungerford put his palms down on his desk, and by unseen hydraulics we stood up from our seats. Wendy began to walk out. I had opened the door when Hungerford asked, "By the way, Haggerty, what are you doin' in my town?"

I askd Wendy to wait outside for me and told Hungerford about Herb Saunders and Justin Randolph and that Sergeant DeVito would hopefully be coming down, or at least contacting him. As I listened to myself repeat the chain of connections, it occurred to me to ask it there'd ever been any crimes like the Saunders' case in this area. Hungerford said, "Not to my memory, but if your time frame is correct, Randolph's been coming down here since before I'd become chief."

"Are there records available?" I asked.

He said, "They're at the county courthouse being programmed into the new computer system set to start up in the fall."

Hungerford tapped his pen against his teeth and pushed his intercom button. "Elsie, we got any iced tea left in the kitchen?"

"Yes, Chief. You want some?"

"Yeah. And none of that no-sweet or whatever. Two lumps of sugar. Thank you.

"I don't usually use her as a gofer, but sometimes I think she listens in on the intercom. Her nosiness saved your butt, but I'd rather she not hear what I've got to say next.

"Instead of going over to records, you ought to go see the guy who was chief before me, Clete Boswell. I took over after he resigned last year. I came here from a stint with the state over in Asheville. You'll find Boswell down at the charter boat docks. He runs a Bertram 31 called *Pot-O-Gold*. How he got that boat's part of why he's not chief any more. Don't tell him I sent you because I'm the other part of why he's not chief, and we don't get along. But he loves to tell stories about his glory days, and if there's anything that happened here like you say went on in Virginia, he'll remember it and embroider the facts all to hell. Somewhere in his bullshit there'll be a fact or two you can use.

"One last thing, Haggerty. I wouldn't worry about those hyenas, but the boy you caught red-handed . . ."

"DuWayne." I strummed.

"Yeah. DuWayne Bascomb. He's got a brother, Bobby Lee or Bubba. You can't miss 'im. He's big as a bear, twice as ugly, and three times as nasty. Most everybody in this town's afraid of him. Once he beat a man to death right there on Main Street. By the time we got to trial, he was acquitted on self-defense. He's why the scum in the bar try crap like this. I've lost more witnesses to more crimes, seen more guilty bastards walk in this town than I can shake a stick at. He's got a hell of an imagination and no conscience. Whatever people claim the other jerks have done, he promises them something worse, custom designed, just for them. So they shut up and let it go. Petty theft, assaults, extortions, vandalism, cars crashed in joyrides, beer stolen. He just lays around like an old she-bear in the dark. The cubs are running amuck, but everybody steps light. This time they might have gone too far.

"With DuWayne involved he might come after you and do something himself—make a mistake. We might catch the old bear this time. Maybe if he comes calling, you'd call me?

Give me something I can make stick." His eyebrows were suspended in hope.

"He comes calling, I'll take a message. Let me ask you one question. Are you afraid of him?"

Hungerford searched himself. "That isn't the point. He isn't afraid of me."

"Well, until then." I knocked off a salute and left. Hungerford didn't look happy.

I picked up my property at the front desk. Wendy was sitting by the front door. I went up to her. She stood up and we went out together.

"We came in together, I wanted us to walk out together."

I smiled at her. "Nice thought." We walked down the steps to our cars. Wendy fished out her keys, hefted them, and looked at me. "Listen, I heard what you said about not having a place. How about staying at my folks' house? It's got three bedrooms. It's the least I can do. I owe you a lot."

"You don't owe me anything, and thanks. But I'm here on a case actually. I probably ought to stay here in town." I was trying to figure out how to deal with Bubba Bascomb's expected visit.

"Look, it's not just that I owe you, but I'm really frightened and would rather not be alone. And you're the only person I know in this town. Or at least the only one I know I don't hate." She said it quietly and with a finality that I knew she wouldn't ask again.

I had a hard time saying no to her and I wasn't entirely happy with that fact. "All right, and thank you."

She smiled at me and turned up the blue in her eyes.

I got in my car and followed her out of the police lot through the main intersection in town and down the beach road past the clinic and the bar. As we went past the bar, she slowed slightly and tossed a small brown bag of trash over the roof of her car. The contents flew out and rained over the lot. She sped up and we went away from town. After a couple of miles she slowed and blinked a right turn. I followed past a sign: Seabreeze Estates — A private beach community. We went through a gate and turned left down the driveway. On our right half-a-dozen beach houses stood on pilings like storks peering over the dunes at the sea.

They were identical homes: weathered gray boards with wraparound decks and skylights. There was a center court-yard to the development with a swimming pool, bathhouses and showers, and inground gas grills. All the houses were well landscaped. We pulled up to the point house of the phalanx. Wendy stepped out and looked at it.

"Looks pretty nice. Let's go in. I have to get it checked out before my folks arrive."

I stepped out and looked at the grounds, dunes, decks, and doors and saw escape routes, high grounds, points of entry. I wasn't real happy at all. I reached in for my suitcase and then went up the steps to the front door. I walked in and put down the case. Wendy stepped by me and went out to bring in the rest of her stuff. Standing in the foyer, I began a security check. To my left, the first floor laundry room. Before me, a kitchen window with a pass-through to the deck. Sliding glass doors off the dining room and living room. I went down the corridor. To the left, a bathroom, no windows; to the right, two bedrooms with windows and skylights, and damn close to the deck railing. I retraced my steps and went up the spiral staircase to the crow's nest upper bedroom. No door at all. Wonderful. A skylight and private balcony. The architect must have used Catburglar Construction Company on this job.

"Excuse me." Wendy came past me and put some things in the bathroom off the bedroom. She came back.

I put up a hand to stop her. "Look, I'm going to call some-one to come down and help me. I've got to find the guy I came here for and keep an eye out to make sure nobody tries to scare us off from pressing charges."

"Do you think that'll happen again?"

"Yeah, I do. In fact, Hungerford just about guaranteed it. That's why I'm calling this guy to backstop me. Can he stay here if he comes down?"

"Is he a friend of yours?"

"Yeah, I like him. I don't know if he 'likes' anybody. But I'd trust him with my life."

"That's good enough for me."

I went over to the bedroom phone and dialed.

Three rings later, "Hello, Bethesda Guns."

"Sandy? This is Leo Haggerty. Arnie around?"

"Sorry, Leo. He went hunting with Mike and Happy Jack. They left yesterday."

"Shit. When's he due back?"

"Saturday."

"Any phone up there?"

"No. They're out in tents."

"Do you know where?"

"No. Wintergreen's a pretty big state park, Leo."

"Shit. If he calls at all, tell him to call me at this number." I read it off the phone to her. "Tell him it's real important. I needed him here yesterday. Okay?"

"Will do, Leo. Good luck."

Everything was going to hell. My ace in the hole had gone off to play his own hand. I was going to have to decide to make him a partner. Or rather, to make him an offer. He'd said he'd never work for anyone and he only took my jobs if they interested him. I tried to think of who else I could call. Arnie was in a league by himself.

There was one other person who'd do a good job. I rang him.

"Reverend Brown's Church of Divine Intervention and Street Justice."

I knew for a fact that this church worker looked like Donna Summers' sexier sister. "Is Shafrath Brown or Wardell Blevins in?"

"Reverend Brown is in. May I say who's calling, suh?"

"Tell him it's Leo Haggerty calling."

"Yes, suh." I went into electronic limbo and waited.

"Leo, blood. What's happening?"

"I'm up to my ass in alligators, Rev. That's what."

"What you need?" He chuckled.

"I need some backup. Give you a chance to terrorize a bunch of crackers. You and Blevins can do your Mau Mau routine."

"Where you at?"

"Cowpie, North Carolina."

"You shittin' me?" He said punintentionally.

"Yeah. It's Bogue Beach, North Carolina. A little beach town."

"Okay. Sounds good. What's in it for me?"

"Five hundred a day."

"Sheeit. That per man, right?"

"Total."

"I don't do charity work."

"Seven fifty, Brown. That's it, and all the ribs you can eat."

"Hey, that's white of you, bro. All right. When do we be there?"

"Now. ASAP."

"No can do, Leo. I'm out five gees on a bond. Broke my own rules. Cunt was a working girl. Should'a knowed better, but she had legs up to her throat. Twitch her buns like a pair of maracas. Woo-wee. I gotta find her first, Leo. That's my bread I'm out. She in town, I'll find her in forty- eight hours max."

"What about Blevins?"

"He's with me on this one. The girl was one of Fat Rufus'

chippies. He's got bad manners. Blevins be Emily Post, heh heh."

Piss. "All right." I repeated the number. "Call me if you're free. I'll tell you how to get here."

"Be seein' ya."

I sat on the bed looking at the ocean, wanting it to carry me away from here. I had to go look for Justin Randolph and Herb Saunders and keep them apart. And keep Bubba Bascomb away from Wendy. Unless we had an immediate breakthrough in cloning, I'd have to keep her with me. Well, she'd be an extra pair of eyes. I shoulda done better at school. You were right, ma. What can I say. There was a hand on my shoulder. "I'm gonna take a shower. Try to get clean. Anything I can get you?"

"No thanks. We'll talk when you get out."

Chapter 14

HERB SAUNDERS HAD LET HIS FINGERS DO THE WALKING ALL day. All he had to show for it was a colossal phone bill and some few facts of omission. Justin Randolph had no telephone, did not subscribe to the local paper, and did not use his house as a rental property. The banks and utility companies refused to talk to him. The office of land records had no record of a sale in 1977 to a Mr. Justin Randolph. The girl had patiently told him, that Randolph could have also bought it under a corporate or foundation name and the officers or at least the managing trustee would be listed and there were no such listings either for that name. Her final bit of good news was that while Bogue Beach was a small incorporated area, the unincorporated areas for ten miles to the west used it as a mailing address and the property could be located out there. And if so, the records wouldn't be here, but in the county seat, sir. Saunders was barely able to thank her. A repeat performance at the county seat only left him with the clear understanding that Randolph did not want anyone to know that he was here.

It wasn't until three o'clock that Herb Saunders realized with a start and a smile that he was in this town as a history lesson. And if that was true, perhaps Justin Randolph was here for the same purpose.

Saunders splashed some water on his face, grabbed his note papers and pen, and after confirming the address, went to the public library.

The library was a small one, and the only one. After asking for the reference section and receiving directions to that area, he found himself standing before a woman concentrating intensely over a crossword puzzle. Saunders cleared his throat, "Ahem. Excuse me, but I wondered if you might help me?"

She looked up at him, but he could tell she was still half-thinking about the puzzle. "Yes?"

"I'm a writer researching the history of eastern North Carolina. I wonder if you'd be so kind as to get me the town newspapers dating back to 1977."

"Oh, my lord. Do you want every issue? That would be thousands. Is there anything in particular you're looking for?"

Saunders wavered between telling her, a move that might save precious time, and plugging on in secrecy so that no one could later connect him with Randolph. That was a concern only if he caught up to Randolph. He tried another approach. "Is there a yearly index for the paper?"

"Why yes, there is. Let me get it for you." She pushed back her chair and disappeared into an alcove. When she returned she held a large book out to him. "Here you go. There isn't one for 1981 on. This is the 1975 to 80 index. If I can do anything else to help you, please ask."

Saunders thanked her and went to a nearby table. Under a slow turning ceiling fan and a clock that went too fast, he searched for the records of an unsolved horror. Looking under CRIME, POLICE, DEATHS he turned up nothing that leaped to his attention. He slowly pushed the book closed and as the pages fell together, he could feel Randolph, and further off, his daughters, slipping away from him down that ever-diminishing crevasse. The thought was paralyzing, the task too big, and for the first time in years Herb Saunders began to cry.

He had not chosen his seat with an eye for seclusion, and his crying, as muffled as it has been, brought attention to him.

Herb pressed down on his eyelids, wiped his nose, and

looked up to see the librarian sitting next to him. "Sorry," he said. "I don't know what came over me."

She smiled. Whether it was empathy or pity he couldn't tell. "Did you find what you were looking for?"

"No. I didn't." And with that he half-told her why he was there. "Actually, you see, I'm not a writer, I'm a detective. I'm here looking for similarities between a case I'm on and something that might have happened here a long time ago. Frustration, I guess, or just one dead end too many got to me."

The librarian clamped her hands on the table in front of her and asked him what he was looking for. After all, she'd lived in this town all her life. Without hope, Saunders said, "I'm looking into the disappearance of children in this town, since 1977. Anything unsolved, where the kids were never found. Not runaways or kidnappings, but stolen — gone without a trace."

The librarian sat back and as she did, Saunders saw her name tag: Mrs. Titus. Her sandy blond hair was shoulder length and turned under with a straight line of bangs low across her forehead. He was sure that had been stylish once, but he couldn't remember when. Neither could he remember when he'd last noticed or thought about style or its absence. Her face was composed like a geometry lesson. The thin line of her nose neatly bisected the perpendicular and equally thin line of her mouth. Riding low on that nose were a pair of wire-rimmed glasses. Saunders saw the same intensity on her she'd shown doing the crossword puzzle.

"You know, this is a small town. I can't think of any disappearances like that, where the kids were never found."

"Okay, what about unsolved crimes against children, murder or rape. It would be something horrible. You'd remember it." Herb wondered whether children had always been the victim. All of the Ripper's disciples had been killers of women.

The only thing he knew for sure was that the crimes were unsolved.

"When you say that, the first thing that comes to mind is the Bryson boy."

"Tell me, tell me." The phoenix of hope was testing its ash-laden wings.

"Let's see. It was about the time you were looking for, late 1977, I think. David Bryson disappeared. There was a ransom demand though, if I remember all this right. Well, the parents both went with the money to where David was supposed to be. Nobody ever showed up. His parents went home. They were just crushed. Well, they got home and there was David. I mean they thought it was David. They saw a boy sitting on the swing in their yard and it looked like David. Apparently they ran across the lawn to him thinking he was okay. They were crying and everything. But when they got to him, they saw that he was dead. His body had been propped up with wires to stay in the seat. It was terrible." A shudder went through Mrs. Titus. "It was clear that the ransom was a ruse to get everyone out of the house. Whoever it was never intended to return the boy. That's the only thing I can think of that's like you described."

Herb Saunders could see Randolph's handiwork in the Bryson boy's death. "Where does the Bryson family live?"

"Oh, they don't live in town any longer. A couple of years later they moved. Back to her hometown. She was from Rocky Mount, I believe. I'm really not sure."

"Was anyone else involved or contacted by the killer that you know of?"

"Let me see."

Saunders stewed in his own juices.

"Well, there was one other person. The Bryson's priest. He organized a lot of the efforts to help them. He made appeals to the killer. I think he even spoke to him, but I'm not sure."

"What church was that?" He was getting to his feet.

"Uh, Holy Redeemer." She was startled at his move to leave.

"Thank you. You've been very helpful." With that he abruptly turned and hurried from the library. Mrs. Titus thought him a strange man. Whatever he had said, she was sure he was also something other than he claimed.

Chapter 15

FATHER SHANNON STILL HAD NO IDEA HOW THE MAN HAD FOUND him. Was there an aura, a stench he gave off? But then the man had seemed possessed, inflamed, perhaps, with a heightened sensitivity to the presence of evil. He came in the late afternoon and pulled off the road with a screech. He strode into the church clutching a black bag. One of the volunteers met him and got the priest. They said a man with wild eyes, a stranger, wanted to see him. Father Shannon went to meet him. The stranger radiated energy compressed into himself. A star on the edge of going nova. Later, Father Shannon pressed his eyes closed and the entire scene would reappear as fresh as the instant it occurred. It was a brand upon him.

"May I help you?"

"Have you spoken to him?"

"I'm sorry, I don't understand what you're saying."

"Bullshit. This is his lair. This town. He contacted me, so he'd contact you. About the Bryson boy. You're the only one left. The family's gone. He's feeding off all of us. Digging up the past, feasting on it. He needs us. It's the only thing that makes any sense." The stranger calmed down in the presence of the priest's bafflement. "That's why the sermon. Out there. I saw the sign: The Devil in Our Midst: Drawing Strength from Evil." His voice grew even calmer trying to ease the priest into an alliance. "You're marked. You can't contain it. It's too much. That's why you need to share it. Tell me where he is. Let me help you. I know. Don't you see. I know. He touched me. He took my girls. I'm here to get them back. Help me."

Father Shannon looked away. "I'm sorry. I don't know what you mean."

"You do. I know it. You can't look me in the eyes. You know I'll see the truth. You're afraid of him. I'm not. I fear nothing. I can help you. Let me. Tell me where he is. I can bring him down. Stop his reign."

"I can not help you. I just can't." Shannon was pleading.

"Why not? You're a man of God. He's the devil."

"He's not the devil. He's a man. He's still one of God's children." Shannon's voice grew even quieter. He was exhausted just finding the words, and they escaped him without conviction.

"We're *all* God's children. He's a cannibal, a wolf in the flock. Give him to me."

"I can't. I took a vow unto God."

"To do what? Hide the enemy? You've broken your vow already. You've told me he's here and he came to you. Give me the last little bit. Where is he?"

"I can't. I've said too much already. I must protect the confessional. He came to me to repent. To confess. To find his way back."

"Bullshit. You fool. He's using you. He's dumping misery everywhere he goes. Leaving piles of it on people like shit, watching the flies gather. You're the shepherd of God's flock. Why do you embrace the wolf?"

"I cannot betray the trust. There is a spark of God in him. He's a human being, no matter what he does."

The man shook his head and growled, "Father, there are sheep and there are wolves. A shepherd who can't tell them apart is no shepherd at all."

"We must help him find that spark within himself. The spark of God in him may be hidden, but not extinguished."

The man's teeth were clenched. "There's no human essence that can't be destroyed. To be a human being is an achievement, and some people just don't make it."

"I'm sorry. I can not judge a man like that. That is God's prerogative."

The stranger roared, "Your god, old man. I won't sacrifice my children on your god's altar. No way. How can you do this? There are innocent children at stake here. He's a monster."

"God has said the confessional is sacred, holy. No matter what the cost, it can not be betrayed."

Louder still, "Your god, not my God. Not my children. Why must they suffer for your beliefs?"

"He's not *my* god. He's my *God.* It's my faith. Even our confusion is his will. It is not my choice; it is my faith. I believe, no matter what things appear to be. If I abandon my faith I have nothing. Not now when it is so hard. I must hold strong or my faith is nothing. I can not believe only when it is easy. I believe this is God's will, that no matter how awful things seem, they are in the service of a greater ultimate good. My duty is clear. I have no choice."

"Of course you have a choice. This side of a pine box there's always room for choice, no matter how cramped the quarters get. You choose your faith at the cost of other's lives. Is the doubt so painful? Climb down here with us who don't have an answer, who are searching."

"I doubt, of course I doubt. Don't you think I care? Don't you think I've looked everywhere for an answer? I am a priest. I can not betray my vows. I believe this is God's will. It is a test of faith, and he has shown the way. I must cleave to it."

"You could give up being a priest. God will survive the loss, I'm sure. Help me save some lives."

"I just can't. This is my relationship with God. I can't answer to men for it. It is between God and me. I wish it were otherwise. Believe me, I do."

"You'll get your chance, Father." The man aimed his finger at him. "Mark my words: study your saints well, Father. You'll soon be among them. I'll let nothing stand between me and my girls. Not you, not your God. I'll trample you to get to them if I have to. That's my god, Father, my faith, my duty." The wild man turned and left the church. The door slammed hollowly behind him and echoed in the vast, silent chambers of Augustus Shannon's heart.

Chapter 16

THE MAN PULLED HIS CAR UP OPPOSITE THE CHURCH AT 4:40 with a predator's precision. When your prey is fleet, timing is of the essence. The priest did not appreciate the urgency of his mission. A lesson needed to be learned. The after-school church class would be dismissed soon as the church schedule on the front lawn promised. He waited patiently. The children flooded out from the church, the first ones met by their waiting parents who had places to be in a hurry. The rest broke off into groups in all directions. Then the torrent was a trickle, the last few stragglers of the flock, the lambs of God.

He saw the one he wanted: a boy, carefully dressed. He was flipping pages of music. He would be a name, a face, a voice, a smile, a tousled head, a beloved pupil, a memory, and a dream.

The boy looked up and squinted into the sun, straightened his books, and bounded down the stairs. He walked up the tree-lined main street to the corner and turned left. The man in the car smiled. A man's gotta do what a man's gotta do. And he thought: *Let's see what your faith is now, Father.*

He started the car, moved up the street, and then turned left, smoothly closing the gap between him and the boy. He pulled alongside, his window down, and said, "Excuse me, son, I wonder if you could help me. I'm trying to find the Beaufort Restoration. I seem to be a bit lost." He picked up the map on the seat next to him, slid the open end of the handcuffs into his other palm, and freed the icepick from its cork tip. The boy walked over to the car, and as the man held the map out to him, he traced the route he wanted on the map.

He heard the click, but never knew what hit him.

Chapter **17**

THE SUN WAS SETTING SLOWLY BEHIND ME, AND I SIPPED MY gin and tonic while I watched the waves roll on forever. Wendy had been sitting alone in her room most of the afternoon. I'd told her that if she wanted to talk about it, I'd listen. It wasn't my forte, but I'd do my best. She passed, saying she wanted to be alone. I was just sitting and measuring the bucket of shit we were in from all directions, first in meters, then feet. Soft footsteps approached. Wendy pulled a chair up next to me and began looking at the ocean.

Looking straight ahead, she began to talk to no one in particular. "I can't stand to be alone. I thought I'd just put my mind to work on it. You know, discipline, and sort out why this happened, how I feel, what I'm going to do." She chuckled sadly, wrapping her long fingers around a cup of tea—or bourbon. "It's just not going anywhere. I thought I'd feel better when I cleaned up. I used a kitchen scrubber even. No way. I feel dirtied in a way soap can't even touch." She set her jaw. "I'm so damn angry. I could kill those bastards, every one of them. Slowly, painfully, horribly, like what they did to me. That scares me. Where did this anger come from? I mean, I know why, but it's so huge. It scares me to want to hurt someone so badly.

"Then I get depressed. Everything feels so hopeless. I have no energy. That's how I felt there on the floor. I just wanted it to end. Any way. I didn't care how. I just gave up. I couldn't fight back anymore." She looked away from me and took a sip, a gulp, and then drained the cup. "I think that's what's hardest for me. Not that it happened, but that there was a point when I didn't care anymore. They could have done anything they wanted to me. I just wanted to die, for it to be over. I gave up. They got me to give myself up. I don't know if I can undo that." She stood up and turned back into the house. "Dammit." She whirled and hurled the mug at the wall.

I put my hand out to her, "Wendy, listen. I don't know if you can either. I do know it takes a long time and I do know that there's no one that can't be broken. It took seven of them all night to do it. You didn't give yourself up easily. The bastards had to take it from you. You stayed alive to fight back, to live again. To rebuild yourself. Hold on to your life, to your future. Rebuild yourself. They tried to destroy you. You can still beat them."

"It shits to be alive. When I wanted to die, when I hoped to die, everything was unbearable. When I survived, when I'd made it, now I look back and wonder was it really so terrible? Couldn't I have fought harder? Made them kill me first?"

"They would have. You did the best you could."

She glanced at me. "Did I? Did I really?" She stalked back into the house. I wondered if she was angry that I'd rescued her. Maybe a bit. I could live with that. I hoped she could.

The gin couldn't cut the bitter taste in my mouth. I remembered coming home after Frankie O'Connell had beaten the shit out of me. My father stood there looking down on me, hands on hips, while I tried to explain that Frankie was two years older. He said with the calm of implacable certainty, "It's not the size of the dog in the fight. It's the size of the fight in the dog." He turned and walked into the house and left me with a slamming screen door for company. I'd taken a lot of beatings trying to live up to those words. As easy as my answers came for Wendy, I knew I'd still try to find out how big a dog I was, no matter what. I was a good-sized fool. That I knew.

It was getting darker. I needed to talk with Wendy about security and what to expect in the next few days. I got up from the chair and walked in toward the kitchen. Curled up on the chair like a big cat, she had a new mug. It was full.

"Do you want something to eat?"

"No. I can't eat."

"What have you got there?" I nodded.

"Gin and Drano."

"What?" I started to grab for the cup. She twisted away.

"It's not. It's just something to make the merry-go-round slow down. All the ugly feelings: being afraid, angry, ashamed. It's bourbon, that's all." She took another slug. "Do you want to eat?" she asked without enthusiam.

"Not really, I guess, but my appetite's nearly indestructible. There's got to be good seafood here in town. We could buy some if a market's still open or go eat out."

"I don't want to be out with people. You could get something and cook it here."

"Okay. We'll talk while we ride." I put down my glass and shucked my empty holster. Wendy was wearing shorts, sandals, and a hooded sweatshirt pulled tight around her face. She'd put on fresh bandages and some makeup over her bruises. I put on a windbreaker and pulled the door closed behind us. We went in my car.

As we pulled away to town I gave her the news. "Listen, that guy I wanted to come down can't make it. At least not right away. That means we're going to have to stay together. I'm trying to find a man. Actually I'm trying to keep two men apart. Here's a photo of the one I'm looking for." I pulled Saunders' photo out of the glove apartment. "You can be a second pair of eyes for me. He's here in town somewhere, looking for another man. I hope to find him first." I tapped Saunders' picture with my finger. She stared at the picture, completely absorbed by it, taking my request seriously. I pushed in my Rosanne Cash tape, her heartbreak voice my sole concession to country-tinged music.

"The second thing is that the chief said the older brother of one of the guys that raped you is a local badass. He intimidates people who get tired of being pushed around by the punks in town. The chief expected he'd pay us a call. That's my problem. I don't want you straying away from me. I want you close at hand. He'll have to go through me to get to you. Got it?"

"Yeah," she said without enthusiasm.

As we drove along the coast road, the skyline looked like midtown Manhattan. Greedy Gulch. The next time around they'll kill Jesus for a zoning variance at the shore. Developers won't consider a place overbuilt until the continental shelf falls off. I hate it. I've been going to the ocean my whole life for solace and solitude. That's almost impossible to find now unless you can buy your own island. Hell, now I go to New York in August. There's nobody there. You can drive the streets. There's no lines, no crowds. No hustle. It's downright pastoral.

We rode past tower after tower. You can tell their age by their promises. The oldest places boast of ocean front; then the next generation offers ocean view, with and without telescope; and the newest ones offer easy access. There were motels, boatels, and condotels. Apparently you can now buy a piece of a place where you used to steal the towels. Scattered among these pleasure hives for weary urban worker bees were liquor stores, night clubs, bikini ships, surfboard stores, and seafood restaurants.

In an incredible display of restraint the real estate and development agents had all agreed to stay on the sound side lest a square foot of prime sand go unsold. We swung right out of town. I looked up and down the coast. This was the only bridge. A hurricane in high season and you'd have thirty thousand drowned in their own gridlock. The developers only care about getting people to the ocean. So what if they float back to shore packed in brine like so many tins of tuna.

As we reached the mainland, the fishing docks were to our left. Slip after slip of sport boats and then farther down the larger commercial boats. We went down through a well kept, quiet side street to the docks.

"Wendy, look for a boat called *Pot-O-Gold*. It belongs to the former chief of police. I need to talk to him."

"Sure."

I slowed the Camaro down and checked my mirrors. No shadow. We went past a row of tackle ships, boat supplies, a dry dock, fish markets. They were all closed. "Looks like we'll have to go elsewhere for some fish."

"Wait. There it is." Wendy wagged a finger at a boat rolling gently in its mooring. I pulled over the curb, got out, and looked both ways. Still no company.

"Keep the doors locked. I'll be right back. Honk the horn if anyone—I mean anyone—approaches the car."

"Please hurry. I really don't want to be alone. I'm scared." She was breathing shallowly after making that admission. Her face had the slick sheen of anxiety but not yet the pasty look of panic.

"Do you want to come with me?"

"No. I'll be okay. Just don't be long. Okay?"

"I'll be in view the whole time and I'll be quick."

I walked over to the dock, down to the gate, and out to the boat. *Pot-O-Gold* was a beauty.

"Ahoy *Pot-O-Gold*. Anyone on board? Captain Boswell?" Nothing.

"He's not here."

I turned to the voice which had come from my left.

"Where is he?" I was searching for my respondent on one of the other bobbing ships.

"Don't know, but he'll be back tomorrow." I found him two ships over. A tall tanned gentleman with snow white hair, Jacques Cousteau's nose, far too little chin for it, and a drink in his hand. I walked down to him.

"Do you know when he'll be here?"

"In the afternoon. He's got a party in the morning. Are you looking to do some fishing?"

That was a nice idea. Maybe when this was all over I'd stay down an extra day and do some fishing. Maybe ask Wendy if she'd like to. "No, just looking for Captain Boswell."

"Well, like I said, he'll be back tomorrow afternoon. If you change your mind about the fishing, here's my card." He fished in his shirt pocket and came up with a card he held to me. I took it. Captain Ethan Franklin.

"Well, Captain Franklin, I just might. I have some business to attend to first, but thanks." I was growing more uneasy by the minute at the distance between myself and the car. Though I could see Wendy, the marina's spike-topped fence meant I had to go back to the gate to get out. I waved absently at Captain Franklin and jogged back to the car.

I unlocked the door and slid in. Wendy exhaled slowly and said, "Whew, made it. Nobody came near, but a car came by and slowed up a bit as it went by. I couldn't see who was in it real well This smoky glass makes it hard."

"Also hard to see in. What kind of car was it?"

"One of those little Toyota pickups. I wrote down the license tag. Here it is." She tore a piece of paper off a pad and handed it to me. I looked at it, folded it up, and pocketed it. "I'll ask the police chief who's car it is in the morning, and I'll keep an eye open to see if it shows up again."

I turned on the ignition and pulled away from the curb. "Do you like to go fishing?"

"Yeah, I guess so. Why?"

"Just an idea. I was thinking I might go fishing when this is all over. Who knows? I thought you might enjoy it too. We'll see."

I made a U turn and left the dock area the way we came in. "I think we're going to need a grocery store if we're going to eat. We have to find out where the natives go for food. There's only fast food mini-markets on the island."

Two blocks over was the main drag of this town. Huddled together in a six block row were the kind of businesses you find when people stay somewhere longer than a weekend: banks, insurance companies, a pharmacy, a clothing store, furniture and florists, a car dealership, movie theatre, two churches, a book store, and a grocery store. Off in the distance, at the edge of town, you could see the huge storage tanks for the deep-water port.

In one way or another, the sea was the life's blood of this town. It was a lure for the tourists — the ocean as playground; for sport and food they pulled fish from it. Up and down the coast huge ships carried vast loads of raw materials on it. The working ocean: a freeway, unchanged since the Phoenicians sailed it.

I pulled up in front of a grocery. After a quick scan for company, we got out and went inside. "How long until your parents arrive?"

"I don't know for sure. "They said by Saturday at the latest. Why?"

"Just trying to figure out how many days' worth of food to get. Time's at a premium. I don't want to spend too much of it in grocery stores. Anything you see that you like, toss it in the cart."

"Okay. I'll split the bill with you."

"Fair enough."

We wandered through the store tossing things in: milk, eggs, coffee, country ham, grits, Granola, barbecue, coleslaw,

beer, soft rolls, o.j. I remember a previous girl friend's warning about monochromatic diets. All our foods were earth
toned. That couldn't be good for you.

I got some distilled water because along with achingly pretty
girls, mosquitos at dusk, sunburn, and Sunday night traffic
jams, beach towns mean bad water. Wendy spent ten minutes
trying to find some edible fruits and vegetables, then gave
up. It was no wonder they breaded and fried everything.
Judging from the signs on the local restaurants, down here
nouvelle cuisine meant broiled, not fried. I got a wine from
New York, some fresh grouper, and a local crustacean that
I swear the girl behind the counter called a "sramp."

Wendy and I split the tab and drove straight home. We
unpacked the groceries and set about to make dinner. I was
making the coating, and Wendy set the table. She looked up
at me. The gumshoe gourmet, snub-nosed spatula in hand.
Tossing that wing of hair out of her face, she put down the
silverware. "Can I ask you a crazy question?"

"Sure. You might get a crazy answer, though." I turned
the fish over.

"Fair enough." She composed herself.

"Do you think I'm pretty?" She looked away for a second
and then back. "I mean, this is really crazy. Forget it."

"No. Go ahead. I'm listening.'

"I mean, look at me. I'm six feet tall. I weigh almost a
hundred and fifty pounds. When I was thirteen, other girls
got breasts, I got shoulders.

"You know when it all happened I kept asking myself why?
Why? I'm not even pretty. I'm too big. I've got muscles, not
curves. I mean I like myself. I guess I mean I like being what
I am, you know, strong and everything. I mean I guess I've
tried to learn to like that, but, you know, dammit, I really
always wanted to be pretty. Oh shit. This is crazy. Forget it."

"I don't know. Something like this turns your world upside

down. Lots of dusty unused thoughts come tumbling out. What happened there had nothing to do with sex or attractiveness, lust or desirability. They wanted to hurt you, hurt someone. When it comes to hurting a woman, rape is the most hurtful kind of beating."

I turned back to my fish. I got it while it was crisp outside, but still moist. Then I took the hush puppies off the oil and spooned out the coleslaw. The wine was as bad as I feared— what I'd expect if Mogan David went varietal. We ate silently. I snuck a couple of looks at her. She was as Elroy so foully put it, a lot of woman. An imposing presence. I wondered what she'd look like without bruises and bandages. I thought I knew.

"For what it's worth, I think you're pretty."

"Thanks, I guess."

As we ate, she looked at me. "You know I owe you a lot. My life maybe and, I don't know, it's kind of strange having that between us and I don't know you at all."

"What do you want to know?"

"I don't know. I guess everything or anything will do. Who are you, Mr. Haggerty?"

"Who am I? I'm a private detective from Washington, D.C. I'm thirty-five years old, six feet tall, two hundred pounds, brown eyes and hair, left-handed. I know which forks to use and I'm not impressed with that. I like Italian food and Irish whiskey, Bruce Springsteen and Jackson Browne, fast cars and funny women. My body tells me that I'm no kid anymore, and my knees can tell the weather. I've got folks like everybody else and two brothers. I had a sister, but she died when I was too young to know the difference."

"Are you married?"

"No. Never. I'd like to, I guess. Everytime I think I'm putting down roots though, they turn out to be landing gear."

I went on. "At least three times a year I wonder what the fuck I'm doin' with my life. This is one of those times. I'm a registered pessimist. Everything's either black or gray."

"Why?"

"Why what?"

"A pessimist."

"When I was eighteen I wanted to save the world. At thirty I knew I wasn't up to it. Now I'm not sure I can save myself. I'd settle for a good woman, my health, and enough money so I won't have to pawn my dignity when I'm old. So far I'm zero for three.

"I'm less optimistic than Miss DuBois about the 'kindness of strangers.' Outside of family and a small circle of friends, we're all of us strangers to each other, and if humanity is judged by how we treat a stranger we're all in trouble. Evil doesn't surprise me anymore, and goodness looks queerer by the day. I expect nothing from my fellow man and am enchanted by decency. Its mere appearance is heroic."

"That doesn't sound like the man who dragged me out of that bar."

"That's probably true," I conceded. "I try to keep my expectations low. That way all my surprises are good ones. I guess I sound bitter. People still disappoint me. I just don't want me to disappoint me. There's nothing else that matters. Nothing lasts. If you leave without regrets, you've done okay."

"You don't mean that. That's too simple. I mean, those men don't regret what they did to me, but it was wrong."

"Okay, okay. You're right." I thought a moment about what she'd said. "All right. This is how I see it: We all accrue pain in our lives. Most of it's unfair. And when we want to dish it out we do the same damn thing. The ones we hurt are just handy, not deserving. I'm just trying to get off that not-so-merry-go-round. Hurt me at your own risk; otherwise, live and let live."

"But you'd have hurt those men for me?"

"You step in when you see that happening to someone who can't defend themselves."

"Were you in Vietnam?"

"No."

Wendy was slowly assembling me from the scraps her questions had purchased. I had no idea what, if any, floor plan she had.

"That doesn't make sense."

"Yes it does. There used to be a poster 'What if they gave a war and nobody came?' If everyone just took care of their own hurt, we'd do okay."

"But you helped me."

"Look, I don't join groups real well and I take orders worse. That's why I wasn't in Vietnam and it's why I'm not married."

Damn. Vietnam. The moral litmus paper of my generation. Imperialism then is patriotism now; and conscience becomes cowardice. What the fuck am I doing explaining myself to a twenty-year-old? Remembering that that's what they said to me fifteen years ago.

"Vietnam was a bad war. We had no business being there. Just like Lebanon or El Salvador now. I believed that then and I do now. Most of the misery in this world is done in the name of good — we're going to do this for your own good. The bigger the cause the more the nitty-gritty reality of people gets sandpapered away. All that bullshit aside, I wasn't going to die for something I didn't believe in. It's as simple as that. But I sure as hell believed you were hurting kid. Lying on that floor, sobbing. You were real to me, anyway."

"But . . ."

"That's it. Class dismissed. Case closed. I don't know how we got off on this shit, but I've had it." I pushed back my chair, stood up, and went out on the deck. I didn't need this shit. She could fend for herself. I'd get a room and get on with business. In the morning she could get another man out here. She had money. There had to be an agency around here. New Bern, maybe.

She was standing behind me in the doorway. "Mr. Haggerty,

listen, I'm sorry I was so — I don't know — picky. I think I was looking for a fight. Maybe I was trying to get you to leave. I don't know. Maybe that's what you were talking about: I was hurt and angry and you were handy. It's not just that, though."

Her pause drew me back around to face her.

"I feel real dependent on you, real vulnerable, and that feeling just makes me sick to my stomach. And I know it's because you're a man. I mean, I look at your hands and I feel their hands on me. I trust you. I mean I want to. Hell, I have to, and I know you haven't hurt me. But what if you turned on me? And I'm angry, angry at all of you, and I'm also grateful to you, and I can't seem to tolerate those two feelings. It has to be one or the other. No, that's not right. It goes back and forth from one to the other. That's all. I just want you to know I'd feel a lot better if you stayed."

I was going to stay, I knew it.

"I'm here for the duration, Wendy. Don't try to sort it all out at once. This is very artificial. There's a lot of instant dependency, intimacy, trust. You have it because of the situation, not by choice. A lot of feelings got stirred up, and we don't know each other at all. Hell, after this is all over you'll probably find that you can't stand me. On a day-to-day basis I can be a real pill. If there's anything enduring to any of these feelings, they'll be there after the dust settles. All right, kid?"

"Yeah. And don't call me kid anymore. I haven't felt like a kid in quite a while."

"Fair enough. I'm sorry. Call me Leo. Mr. Haggerty is my father."

"Okay. Are we friends? I'd like to be."

"Who knows? Maybe we could be. I don't know what we are. We're in deep shit together; and if we make it through, it'll be because we helped each other. Friends do that. So maybe, after this is all over, we'll find out. If need gets replaced by choice we'll be friends. Right now we're allies. I'd like to be friends, too. So put that thought in some place safe until this is over."

We went in and put away our dishes. I poured out the rest of the wine. "Listen, we need to discuss security here for a moment. I wish it wasn't that way, but we're just out of jail, not out of the woods. Part of my attention is going to be diverted into looking for this guy, so you'll need to contract a case of instant paranoia, at least until I can get some help. I've looked around and this place isn't terribly bad. Use the peephole whenever you go the the door. You don't go anywhere without me and vice versa. There's good exterior lights on this project and a dead bolt on the front door. I want you to sleep upstairs. Keep the phone by your bed. You hear any noise from me, get on the phone. If the lines are cut, go out on your deck and yell like hell. Yell 'fire.' People'll wake up for that. I also want you to take a kitchen knife up with you. I'll sleep down here. The glass doors have charley bars and they're pinned nicely, but if Godzilla's as subtle as Hungerford promised, he'd rather come through the door than open it. Okay?"

"Yeah. Okay." Wendy dumped her dishes and went up the spiral staircase. Halfway up she stopped. "Good night, Leo, and thank you . . . for everything. It really doesn't feel like enough for what you've done."

"Listen, I know how you feel and I appreciate you don't take lightly what I did. But in some ways, just like those guys, it had nothing to do with you. I didn't know you when I stepped into that bathroom. You were a stranger to me. I did it for all the unearned kindness I've had in my life. Hold on to that feeling. Someday, somewhere, you'll be in a position to help a stranger who needed it like you did. It'll be your chance to put something back in the pot. Don't be in such a hurry to pay off that debt. If it's important, do it right. Anyway, go to bed and try to sleep."

She waved a small good night and went up the staircase so slowly it looked as if she were pulling herself and not climbing up the stairs.

I pulled the Bushmills out of the bar, poured a jigger full, and went out and balanced it on the deck railing. Then I opened up my suitcase and there and then began to contravene Chief Maxwell Hungerford's cherished wishes. I unwrapped my sawed-off Remington 870 pump gun and stroked and oiled it to the ocean's roll. Cool sea breezes braced me. The Bushmills stoked my furnace. In the distance the freighters waiting their turn to unload at the Morehead City port lay at anchor on a careful line through the Shackleford Straits. Closer at hand the sea oats waved, and beyond them the lights on the city fishing pier went on. The beach was deserted. I looked over the railing at the scrub pines, then up to the deck of Wendy's bedroom. I was afraid they'd bypass the first floor and just go up to her deck. A smart man would.

I slipped the magazine extender on the pump gun. It hung out like a Hapsburg's lip. I went through my shot shells. I didn't intend to fuck around with these assholes. I counted out my fléchette rounds. Two hundred fiberglass needles per. One of these upclose and personal and you look like the cover on a Whitman Sampler. They're X-ray opaque to boot. I thought they were fitting. If you don't die right off, you get to lie around for a couple of months waiting, hoping they'll migrate to the surface. Once they're in you, there's nothing you can do about it, but just wait until they come out on their own accord. Kind of like rape. I loaded three rounds of fléchette and filled the extender with double-ought buckshot loads. I hoped they didn't have grappling hooks and would just climb up. I'd give a lot for a good vibration sensor. I put the TV on while I rigged a homemade alarm.

I went into the kitchen and got a bunch of soda cans, some clothesline, and loose change. After emptying the cans, I punched holes in them, tossed some coins in each one, and threaded the clothesline through.

Late night TV was getting pretty strange. I rolled past the reruns of *Celebrity Paternity Suit*. Something called *Meet Your Maker* was on. It looked like a necrophile's fantasy island. Boy George was singing "do you really want to hurt me" to Mike Hammer. I don't think George liked the answer. Then again, maybe he did. I couldn't handle anything that subtle anymore.

The telephone went off like a shot. I killed the TV, picked up the phone, and said nothing.

"You Haggerty?" I didn't say anything.

"Listen good. I'll only say this once. You don't forget this foolishness you've stirred the chief up with, I'm gonna see that DuWayne gets to finish what he started. And you'll get to watch. That is I'm gonna make sure you do soon's I finish cuttin' off your eyelids."

The line went dead, and I hung up the phone. Bubba was an occidental fool. The obligatory warning. The western way of war. The "rules" of war. The idea of war was to win. No matter how. Never threaten, just deliver. If we'd understood that Pearl Harbor never would have happened. If they'd understood us, they never would have done it.

I wanted to go right out after him and just shoot the bastard in an alley, but I couldn't. I'd have to wait until he came to me and then counterpunch him to death. I didn't foresee reasoning with Bubba.

Anxiety numbed my fingers, and it took ten minutes to finish stringing the soda can line. I went out on the deck and found hooks already in the corners. The clothesline would be for drying bathing suits. The cans sat just below the railing grip. Anyone or anything hooking over it would rattle them and awaken me. So I hoped.

I picked up the pump gun and turned into the house. A figure moved. I lifted the gun.

"Jesus, don't shoot! It's me," Wendy shrieked.

"Goddamn. I thought you were asleep."

"I couldn't. I heard the phone. I picked up the extension. I just couldn't go back to bed."

"Come on down then." I lowered the gun.

"What are you gonna do? I can't take this. My god, when is it going to end?" She was starting to twitch. Reflexively she hugged herself to stop the shaking.

"Good question. I don't know. But until it does I'm gonna keep a close watch on you. Hope for backup. Pray for rain. Keep a high profile in town and hope like hell I find Bubba first. I'll take him out if I can, then do the job I'm here for."

"I could just forget it, leave town. I'm a nervous wreck. I can't sleep. I see them in my mind, out there somewhere, watching me, waiting for me. I was trying to tell myself it wasn't true, that it was over, I was safe. Then this." She curled up in the chair and began to rock back and forth. "I can end it, just give up. Goddamn." She began to cry, retching gasps.

"No, you can't. That's what they want. Then you'd really feel like you gave yourself up. That's what hurt most, you said. Hold on. Hungerford's a decent man. He'll help us if he can. I'm not superman, but I'm no slouch at this business. I can't give you a guarantee, but if you give them what they want there's no guarantee they'll stop there. You take your chances either way."

She'd continued rocking and crying as I spoke. I had no idea if she'd even heard me. Gradually she stopped moving. She squeezed her eyes shut, a grimace to stop the tears. Suddenly she banged her fist on the table. Through clenched teeth, she said, "Damn. I hate being scared. Shit."

I put my hands on her shoulders. "The best thing for being scared is fighting back. Now get upstairs. Sleep if you can."

She turned away. My palms burned from touching her, and when I swallowed I thought a bow tie had been stapled to my throat. An allergic reaction to my guilty pleasure in the contact. She went into the kitchen and came back with the biggest knife in the house.

I watched her climb the stairs and picked up the pump gun. I pulled a chair around toward the deck and dragged it far enough back to still be in the shadows at dawn. The twelve gauge lay across me like a lap dog. This one's bite was a lot worse than its bark. I slept waiting for a tin can rattle and hoping for the sun.

Chapter 18

I AWOKE TO THE SUN AND WENDY'S GENTLE TAPPING ON MY shoulder. "Easy, it's just me," she said.

"Good morning." I shifted the gun off my lap and stood up.

"How'd you sleep?" she asked.

"I slept. That's all I was hoping for. How about you?"

"I guess like you said, I made it through the night. I dozed off and on. I know I must have dreamt and I'm sure they were bad, but I don't remember them."

I edged around her and went into the bathroom and splashed warm water into my gritty eyes and brushed my teeth.

"Do you want any breakfast?"

"Sure."

"I'll make it. You did dinner."

"Fine." I walked back into the kitchen and slid into a chair. Coffee was on, and Wendy opened the refrigerator, poured me some orange juice, and handed it to me. "Thanks." Our eyes met for a moment, and we both broke off the contact. I wasn't sure why. I was faintly sad and didn't understand that either.

I sipped the juice and looked out at the ocean. As the waves moved to shore, they gathered up the sun's glare, and for an instant it was all one piece, a mirrored sea. Then it fell apart into metallic freckles for a while and finally a flat blue-green finish. As my eye followed each swell to shore the next was already on its way. The seamless sea. The location of the mirror moment changed throughout the day as the sun heaved itself across the sky.

"How do you like your eggs?" Wendy asked, her back still to me, hand poised above the carton.

"Scrambled softly."

"Ham?"

"Yes."

"Grits?"

"Yes."

"I'll do my best with those. I've never made them before."

"Don't worry. I think they're instant grits or quick grits. All the mystery has been processed out of them."

"Whew." She bustled around and in a few minutes I had a plate of scrambled eggs, country ham and grits, and a mug of coffee. Wendy had a glass of orange juice.

"Aren't you going to eat?" I was some detective.

"No. I don't eat breakfast. Usually I go work out first when I get up. Then I come back and eat."

"I'm not sure that's such a hot idea, frankly," I said around a melting mound of eggs.

"Why?" The word was short and unexpectedly sharp.

"Because there's a bunch of guys out there who do not like you very much, and I think staying close to home, in a defensible spot, makes sense. At least until I can get some backup here."

"Then what?"

"Then I go looking for Herb Saunders."

"But if you can't get help, then you need to take me with you, right?"

"Yes, that's right." My ham and grits were no consolation.

"So we'll be out there at risk anyway. I may as well go out and work out. And anyway, I'm your client, right? So if I want you to protect me while I work out, that's your job."

Fortunately she was smiling as she twisted my emergency room lie to her own ends.

"What's the big deal? So you miss a couple of days running on the beach. Do sit-ups or one of those workout shows . . ." One look at her and I felt like I'd called Bubba Smith a nigger.

"The big deal is that the trials are in three weeks, and I've put almost four years of my life into this, and I am not going to let those bastards take that away from me too."

"Right. I'm sorry I took it so lightly. Now just tell me what I took so lightly?" I turned my palms up. The empty hand of peace.

"The track and field trials for the '84 games are only three weeks away. I have a real chance to make the team. I threw sixty-one meters at the PAC-10's." Anger was replaced by earnestness. In a glorified way, she was asking me if she could go outside to play.

"I'm sorry, but my code book has no entries for that last sentence. What did you throw?" I was being unnecessarily thickheaded, but I could feel myself being maneuvered into something I didn't want to do and I wasn't going to make it easy.

"The javelin. I'm sure it's going to take a sixty to sixty-five meter throw to win. I can do it. I can feel it."

I sipped coffee and stroked my mustache.

"Look, you're the one who said fighting back was important. Well, this is an important part of my life, and if I don't go out and stay as sharp as I can because I'm afraid, then I'll have lost even more than I already have. This may be my only chance. This may be the last Olympics. I'm sore as hell, and I probably can't tie my shoelaces I'm so nervous, but there are some things I can still do."

I had the feeling the discussion was over. I sipped. I stroked. I delayed. What if she said she'd go out without me? Would I hog-tie her and lock her in her room? What if I had to go out and take her with me afterward? "All right, let's make a deal. If I can get someone down here to be with you, you hold off the workouts until they arrive. If I can't, then I'll go out with you. We'll do it this morning before Captain Boswell's charter comes in. Fair enough?"

"Fair enough. Go make your calls." She had a big smile on. Her first victory at the beach.

I maneuvered the remnants of my breakfast around with my fork like a hockey player killing a penalty, then finished it with a scoop shot into my mouth. With a refill on the coffee, I went to the phone in the living room. Two brief and disappointing calls later I knew that Arnie was still in the woods, the Rev was on the streets, and I was going to track practice.

"Okay. Let's go. Spear chucking time." I was still miffed.

"Watch it. You might just catch one by accident." Wendy laughed as she went upstairs to change. I was glad to hear that sound. As she dressed I tried to figure out how to protect her. Actually, working out in an open field wasn't a bad place to be. I'd try to have two exits at least and control access to the area. The major danger was a long-range attack, like a 30.06 at three hundred yards. That could just as easily happen when we walked out the front door. All I could see was hazards. Somebody forgot to put fairways on this course.

I went into the bedroom and got native: deck shoes, shorts, T-shirt, and shades. I took a hat and windbreaker along because they're the easiest way to disguise yourself. I unpacked my binoculars, then unloaded the Remington and inserted solid slug rounds to increase its range. In the living room I wrapped it in the windbreaker and waited for Wendy.

She came out in a Berkeley warm-up suit carrying a gold and white gym bag. "You ready?" she said.

"Yeah. Listen to me, carefully. I'm going to go out first and check the car."

She interrupted, "We'll have to take mine. My javelins are on the roof rack."

"Okay. Give me the keys. If everything's all right I won't

signal you out, I'll get in and start the engine. Come out when you're ready. If everything's not right, you'll know it. Get on the phone and call Hungerford and stay away from the windows."

She nodded understandingly. I went up to the front window and looked out from a corner. The best location for a shot would be behind another car on the lot or from a porch on the houses facing us. Either way, they were looking into the sun. God grant me a flash on a barrel. I scanned once with my binoculars and saw nothing. I felt Wendy's hand slip the keys into mine. I put the Remington in front of me under my jacket and gripped the trigger.

Wendy opened the door, and I slid out down the stairs and across the lawn to the car. Nothing yet. My eyes were everywhere. I got to the car, dropped down to the ground, rolled over, and looked at its underside. Nothing was affixed there. I rolled out, got to a squat, unlocked the door, and released the hood. Still nothing. I duck-walked around to the front end, pulled the hood up between the house and me and the house across the way. Nothing that wasn't put there in Munich. I slammed the hood and scooted around and into the driver's seat. Unlocking a door for Wendy, I started the engine. A three count and she was out the door, down the stairs, and beside me. I backed the car out of its slot and headed out of the development. My chest hurt. I was still holding my breath. I let it out with a rush and shook my head. I flicked my eyes into the rearview mirror and saw nothing.

"Where are we going?" I asked.

"To the high school. I passed it on my way into town. The fields will be free since school's out. It's straight out the main drag on the right-hand side." She sat with her bag on her lap and periodically checked the rearview to see if we were being followed. She played incessantly with her bag's zipper.

Less than ten minutes later we were in front of the high

school. I pulled around the main building, drove past the field
house wing, and parked at the end of the football field.

"Just sit here a minute. I want to take a look around." I
put up a restraining hand and then slid out of the car. I walked
out to the football field with the pump gun still wrapped over
my left shoulder. The stadium had bleachers on three sides.
They looked high enough and close enough to the buildings
to preclude a shot from the rooftop. I jogged over and climbed
to the top to convince myself of that. A military marksman
might have been able to shoot through that mesh of supporting
beams and crosspieces, but I was betting these boys couldn't.
I trotted back toward the car. There was only one way in
or out. I'd park myself where I could see the access road.

"Okay. What are you going to do?"

"Stretches, steps, sprints, practice throws. That's all."

"Okay, use the near end zone or these bleachers here for
your steps and stretches. Sprint on this near side line and
throw from the end zone. If anybody comes in, I'll honk once
and drive to you to pick you up. Don't stop for anything.
Javelin, gym bag, anything. Got it?"

"Yeah. Let me leave my stuff in the car then unless I'm
using it." She got out of the car, opened the bag and dumped
out videotapes marked Lillak, Schmidt, Felke, and Petranoff.
There was also a book entitled *Zen and the Torque Dynamics of
the Javelin* by some guy with a Scandinavian name. She pulled
out a pair of ankle weights, slung them over her shoulder,
and walked away. I started the car and backed up so as to
give me a view of the roadway. With the Remington on the
seat next to me, I sat and waited. Every few minutes I'd toss
a look at Wendy. She spent a good half hour stretching:
hurdler's stretches, toe touches, trunk twists, side bends, sit-
ups, things for her legs, her abdomen and back, arms and
shoulders. She stepped out of her warm-up pants and pulled
the shirt over her head. After a couple of loose-jointed

bounces, she strapped on the ankle weights and ran up and down the bleachers. Then she jumped up the bleachers three steps at a time and ran down. After more leaps than I could do, she ran forty-yard dashes. Crouched in the end zone, she'd explode out for thirty yards and then glide the last ten. Over and over again. That whole morning she was the only person out there. After a while, she walked over to the car, opened the door, took a towel from her bag, and wiped her face.

"How do you feel?"

"Better. Good. I feel like I was starting to get kind of numb all over. Not just emotionally, but like this wasn't my body, it was somebody else's. I didn't like it. I didn't want it. It was spoiled. This helps. I needed to do this. Kind of repossess myself, take over again." She wiped her hands and reached in for a small can of powder she then put on her hands. Next she slipped a white elastic wrap over her elbow. "I'm going to just work on my steps and then make a few easy tosses, just for technique. That'll be it."

"Fine."

She reached up and unsnapped a long cylinder from the roof. With it over her shoulder, she went back to work. I watched the curves of her calves, the sweep of her thighs, up to the broad back and shoulders. She was a strong woman. Men still reacted to that by deciding whether it was attractive to them or not. It was a look that women had been punished for before, so every new possibility reclaimed was a victory. But it was a victory not because it was an added way to be attractive, but because strength itself feels good to the wielder, audience be damned. I remembered my college sweetheart. Lushly female, she sculpted space without a single straight edge. And she moved with an implausible harmony. But she was so soft that when a breeze came up she'd bruise. That was then, this is now. I think I like now just fine.

Wendy was working on her steps. From the goal line she

counted back twenty steps. From her tube she withdrew what looked like a thick black hose with a donut of a nose weight on the end. I turned back to watch the road and saw her practice runs only in disjointed segments. Finally, she slipped out her javelin and walked to the goal line, looking off into space. She turned and began to count off her steps. I opened the car door and got out to watch her. The spear was in her upturned palm right beside her bandaged ear. I squinted into the full midday sun and made a visor of my hand. Everywhere it was still and silent. The empty bleachers, the vacant field.

She started with a dip, rocking back on her heels, and then she was off. With each stride she accelerated, hurtling toward the goal line, building power along the way, storing it in her legs like a battery. Then quickly she changed into a crossover step like a cantering show horse, cocked her arm, took a last little hop, and planted her lead leg. The stored power rose up her legs and churned through her snapping hips. Her universal joint turned thrust into spin. Her left arm swept back a curtain of air and the energy rose. Restraint funneled it up her arched back. Her shoulder resisted then relented. But she didn't throw. Her shoulders turned, her upper arm followed through, but the elbow declined. And still she didn't throw. Her head swiveled up and away searching for something. In that still summer sky she saw a window, the true point that she would throw through. And then it was done.

I looked into the sky, and the javelin was gone. I couldn't find it. It was as if she had thrown it through a doorway into another world. Just when I began to believe that, it fell out of the sky and stabbed the earth.

Wendy had watched and waited for it to land from the goal line. When it had, she gathered up her gear and trotted out to retrieve it. She checked her distance, pulled it from the earth's grip, and slipped it into its sheath.

I was checking out the roadway again when she got to the car, fastened down her javelin, and tossed her gear in the back seat.

"How do you feel?"

"Good. Good. Like I burned something off out there. I can feel all of myself again, my legs, back, arms. I feel real. Here. Right now. I don't know how long it'll last, but it sure beats feeling like a ghost in your own body. When they—"she looked around for the right word, one that was honest, but not catalytic—"hurt me, I just went numb and dead all over. Like I dove down into myself. into cold water and curled up around myself, a tight ball in the dark. This morning I knew they weren't there anymore, but I was still in the dark. All this got me back to my surface. For now at least." She smiled and said, "Let's go eat. I'm starved."

"Okay. Do you like barbecue? It's the state food of North Carolina."

"Sure."

I checked my watch. "We'll get some to go and then head to the docks. Boswell's boat should be in." Turning left out of the school's driveway, we went back to town. On the right was a sign for the Pork Palace. Below that is said: BBQ, minced and sliced, fit for a king. We pulled in and I gave Wendy some money for sandwiches minced with slaw, a bag of hush puppies at six cents a piece, and a couple of beers. Sitting on the car hood, I watched her walk away. I wished like hell I was that young again. I'd settle for problems where a sprained ego was the worst outcome.

Then she was there in front of me. "Whatcha thinkin'? You've been real quiet all morning."

"Ah, nothing. Just tired. Slept like hell."

"Is that all? Even allies need to be honest with each other."

"Is that so? Says who?"

"Says your ally."

"No. That ain't all. I was thinkin' about how pretty you are and how desirable and how I didn't really want to tell you that because you need to hear about men's desires like a hole in the head."

"Oh yeah? You're the one who told me that rape had nothing to do with sex or desire. In fact, it's nice to hear. Part of me wonders if a man would still want me after what happened. You know, if it shows or something."

"This guy would. You look clean and strong, young and pretty. Everything a man could want." I didn't tell her that I'd no more let myself get involved with a twenty-year-old girl than with a twelve-year-old. How much of their attractiveness is their youth? A chance to make a liar out of time, to recapture that golden age that never was. All thirty-five-year-olds would make great eighteen-year-olds the second time around. Get it right finally. How much I ached when I looked at her for my own youth, forever fled. No matter how tightly I'd clasp her to me I'd never get it back. How sweet the desire. But shot through with sadness. You might as well try to nail a board to the sea. I leaned forward and kissed Wendy lightly on the cheek.

She touched her face and looked away. "I'm sorry, Wendy."

"I'm not."

"I'm sorry I'm not twenty, is what. Get in the car."

We climbed in and drove off. I took the sandwich from her and propped the beer between my legs. We were one block off the channel, near the end of the residential area before the sport fishing docks began.

Chapter 19

WE RODE SILENTLY DOWN TO THE DOCK, FOUND A PARKING SPOT in the lot across the street, locked the car up, and walked over to the boats. The wind had come up, and we'd both put our jackets on. Before that though, I'd taken the Remington out of the car inside my jacket and locked it in the trunk. I didn't want some busybody admiring the car or inspecting the javelin tubes and looking in the window, go, "Oh my gosh," and call the police. We strolled down to the docks. Boswell's berth was still empty. I wandered over to Captain Franklin's boat, looked her up and down, and then wandered to the end of the dock. Wendy was tagging along, occupied with her own thoughts. Perhaps she was reviewing her practice throws.

I got to the end of the dock and put a foot up on the top of one of the pilings and looked out at the ocean. For ten years I had fished these waters with my father, from Key West to Montauk Point. We boated shark, marlin, giant grouper. We didn't talk much out there. My dad didn't talk much anywhere. We were just trying to find something to do together where we wouldn't fight. Neither of us wanted me to make a mistake at anything, so he could never teach me anything.

We did learn to spend time together. I learned to drink beer and I learned to fish. I acquired some patience, where I had none. After a few years of sitting side by side all day in the sun sipping beer, squinting at strike signs, we stopped pushing at each other. When my anger had dissipated like a fog, I found underneath a deep still pool of sadness. I knew how hard my dad was trying to reach me, how hard it was for him, and how hard I made it for him. Things got better after that. Then one day, fifteen miles off of Miami, it all came together. I hooked a swordfish and fought him for five hours. My dad harnessed me in the fighting chair. When I got dizzy, he tied a cool cloth around my neck. All afternoon he helped me bring him in and I let him. We were doing it together. It just happened it was my hands on the reel.

At three o'clock that day our fish broke water fifteen feet off the stern, fixed us with that great flat saucer of an eye he had, like he wanted to know if we were ready, and made his last run for it. The line went out so fast the reel was smoking, but we brought him back, wind after wind, pull after pull, foot after foot. At the end though, there was nothing there. The leader had been snapped off clean. I cried out of sadness and relief at losing that fish, but my dad had been everything I wanted that day. He'd been wise when the fish confused me, patient when I made mistakes, enthusiastic when I tired and thought I couldn't go on, calm when I was scared, and just there at the end. We had rough times after that, but we'd made a certain kind of peace on that long afternoon.

Yeah, I'd fished these waters for ten years with my dad until one night in our kitchen his heart blew a big hole in itself. We were talking, and he stood up to get another cigar when his mouth opened and he made a sound like a drain emptying. His eyes rolled, and he turned gray and fell back into the chair. He was stiff and looked halfway gone. I remember looking at him and saying, "Dad, Dad, Dad." That's the last thing I clearly remember, but I must've called an ambulance because one showed up and took him to G. W. Hospital where he pulled through. He never fished again, though, and neither have I. I just never wanted to do that with anyone else. I think maybe I do now, though I don't know why.

I stepped back from my reverie and looked around for Wendy. She'd been right next to me.

"You got kind of spacey, there. Are you sure you're all right?"

"Yeah, honest. I'm sorry. Don't worry about me. I'm all here, on active duty now. Let's go look for Boswell." The half-day charters were coming in, and the dock was filling up. Everyone was milling around trying to see what had been caught and by whom. I took Wendy by the elbow and steered her through the crowds.

He was just there, right in front of me. I almost did a double take. Instead I just walked by and took up a position a few feet away and looked expectantly out to the sea. After a decent interval, as they say, I turned to Wendy and said, "That's him, Herb Saunders. Let's just wait here until he moves off the dock and we can talk to him alone." She nodded and tried to look over my shoulder at him. I turned back and, scrupulously not looking at him, tried to pick up his conversation over the din all around us.

"How much is it?" he said to a leathery skinned bandy-legged old man who looked like a tortoise unshelled.

The man turned away from me and pointed down the dock. He turned back, and Saunders asked him how much time he needed. The guy replied whenever you want, just give me a call first. They shook hands, and the old guy ticked off a salute at Saunders and walked past him and then us. Saunders took the whole scene in one last time, found nothing of interest, and moved to the exit. I had found one thing of interest. There was no black bag.

I thought about his looks and realized I'd never assembled a picture of him in my mind. He was shorter than I, probably five foot nine or so, bushy browed, and bald. I watched his eyes as they scanned the crowds again. The furrow on his brow looked permanent, and he exuded an aura of focused energy. His thick arms, legs, and torso added to the image of energy compacted and intensified.

When he had moved off a little way from the crowd, I began

to close on him. I wasn't sure what was the best approach to take. Confrontation seemed wrong, so I called after him. "Excuse me, sir. Did you drop this?" I held out a ten dollar bill to him. It always works. Everyone stops for a second to recall if they had such a bill or to make sure it's still there. Then there's the extra measure taken to consider the current market value of their integrity. That's all I needed. I was right up next to Saunders when he concluded that it wasn't his and he wouldn't lie for it.

"Hello, my name is Leo Haggerty. Your wife, Maggie, is worried about you, Mr. Saunders. She asked me to look for you." I searched for signs that he was going to hit me or bolt. He just blinked once and said, "Excuse me, but you've made a mistake. My name is not Saunders."

I reached quickly for his picture in my jacket pocket, smiled, and eased it out. "That's you, Mr. Saunders. I'm not mistaken. I'm not the police and I'm not a friend of Justin Randolph's. Your wife hired me to find you. She's quite upset about your disappearance. She thought it was like in the past — you chasing ghosts."

His face flushed with indignation. I continued. "We know why you're here. He's no ghost. I followed your trail to Justin Randolph. So did Maggie and Pete DeVito. I've told the local police. Let them look for him, or get the FBI called in. Or let me look for him. Why don't you go back to Maggie? She needs you."

His expression changed. "No. No more stand-ins. That's the problem with everything today. Nobody does for themselves. We've got experts and consultants on how to wipe your ass. Well, not me and not this. My kids. MY KIDS. Do you hear? I'll get them back." He jabbed a fat forefinger at himself and then me.

"Okay. I can understand that. Let me help you though. Double your chances of finding him. Can you afford not to?"

My offer perplexed him. He rubbed his chin a couple of times.

"No. I'll do it alone. This town's small. He won't escape."

"That isn't it, is it? You don't just want your girls, you want Randolph too, for yourself. If it was your girls, you'd take any helping hand you could find. No, you want some time alone with Randolph. You want vengeance." I didn't feel at all smug.

"So what?"

"So nothing. I don't care what happens to Randolph. I do care about your wife and your kids. They need you, and you're no good to anyone in jail if you kill Randolph."

"I won't kill him unless I have to. And you're only half-right, Mr. High and Mighty. Revenge would suit me just fine. But I want first crack at locating my girls, unhampered by 'due process' bullshit. No sleazebag lawyers, plea bargaining, wheeling in the whore-shrinks, tying up everybody's hands with paper chains. No. Just a simple question and answer session between Mr. Randolph and me."

I thought bitterly that the greatest obstacle to action in our society was a piece of paper entitled "Motion." "I understand how you feel, Mr. Saunders. I'm sure I'd want to do the same thing. But I can't let you. It's not that the law is sacred to me. I've trampled it a few times and tippy-toed around it plenty, but your wife's my client and she wants you back safely. Simple as that. I've got a job to do."

I didn't want to stand too long in his shoes. I didn't want his pain and rage to seep up through me. I'd wind up letting him crucify Randolph and then dance around the body. No. Let me remember Maggie's sad eyes, her pain and loss. There were too many masters here, too many conflicting goals, too many hurts to repair. I had to pick one, yet it was getting ever harder to ignore the others' claim. The lady of the scales is not blind out of wisdom or choice, but out of necessity.

"Let me search for him with you, Saunders. This is my last offer. Otherwise, I'll be on you like a rash. You may find him first, but I won't give you the time you want." Somewhere back in the darkest corner of my mind I held out the hope that if I was with him, maybe something would happen where I couldn't protect Randolph. Then Saunders would get his wish, but it wouldn't be my fault. That was more craven than I could stand, so I buried that thought.

"No. That's my final word. You follow me and that's harassment. I'll call the cops on you. Swear out a complaint."

It was a nice move. "Like hell you will. You don't want the police knowing you're here or where you are. As you said, you want to be left alone. If you don't let me go along with you, I'll call the cops on you." Thrust.

"What for? They can't arrest me for anything. I haven't done a thing. I'm just a tourist. Not only that, in case you haven't noticed, this little burg is starting to fill up fast. By tomorrow there'll be ten or fifteen thousand people here for the weekend. They couldn't watch me if they wanted to." Parry.

We had a standoff. If I tailed him, he'd get my wrist slapped and I'd lose him in the crowds. Even if his pursuit of Randolph was obstructed briefly, he was right. The police couldn't keep him under surveillance. I was betting he wouldn't want even that brief interruption of his hunt.

"I'm calling your bluff, smartass. I'm going to walk. Follow me and see what happens."

I was wrong. Time to regroup, take a new track. I watched Saunders walk away from me. I had an idea, but I couldn't implement it, yet. I looked at Wendy who'd been patiently standing by and motioned for her to head to the car.

As I walked over to the car there was a note under the windshield wiper. I plucked it out and unfolded it. Just three lines.

SLOPPY SECONDS
WHEN YOU LEAST EXPECT IT
SWEET THING

"Damn." Trying to watch out for Wendy and find Saunders had made me as useful as a one-legged man at an ass kicking. I folded it over and calmly put it in my jacket pocket. I didn't ball it up and throw it away. That would be anger. I didn't whirl and look all around for the author. That would be fear and confusion. No, I just went around and let Wendy into the car and then let myself in. That was indifference. The threat was less than an object of my concern. I moved my eyes behind my shades and saw nothing but a large shape slide through the front door of the hardware store across the street. Coincidence perhaps. My pulse was pounding in my ears, but I continued to appear unruffled. As Arnie would say: a threat is a fool's gift, for surprise is one of the four great weapons. I tried to recall his Kenjutsu lesson.

> The blade is unsheathed by the willingness to die
> Each proper blow begins with the surprise that
>   disarms
> Is struck with the ferocity that crushes the will
> And from the stance that keeps each next blow a
>   secret.

They had given away surprise and that was nice. I just needed to work on the "willingness to die" end of things.

Wendy fortunately hadn't paid attention to the note, and I wasn't about to tell her about it. She'd taken a big step back into the world this morning, overcoming her fear to do something that had been part of her "normal" life. This letter, like Bubba's call could undo all that. I backed the car up and slowly rolled after Saunders who was headed toward a motel near the end of the docks. He never bothered to see if I was following him. He just went up to the building, climbed the stairs at the end of it, went down to his room, and entered. I drove around to the back and checked to see if there was a back stairway up to his room. There was. A slow turn through the parking lot turned up three cars with Maryland tags. Two had "Go Terp" bumper stickers and were parked side by side. The third I guessed to be Saunders'. It was right next to the staircase.

It was time for my new approach. I parked in the fire lane so I could use the public phone just outside the manager's office, and still be close to the car if Saunders came running out and tried to get in his car and lose us. Wendy got the job of keeping an eye on the staircase for Saunders' return. I gave the operator my credit card number and waited to hear Maggie Saunders' voice. That wasn't to be. A man answered the phone.

"Uh, hello. I'd like to speak with Margaret Saunders." Keep it cryptic.

"I'm sorry, that's impossible."

I didn't like his choice of words. "Impossible. Why? What's happened?"

"I'm sorry, I can't say anything else. I'd suggest you call the police for further information." The line went dead before I got to say thanks a lot.

I got the same operator and told her the next call was an emergency call to the police and to override any busy lines. She took DeVito's number and put me though.

"Police. This is Officer Shanahan. May I help you?" A mellow-toned copette.

"Yes. Is Sergeant DeVito there, please?"

"May I say who's calling?"

"Yes. It's Leo Haggerty about Herb Saunders."

"Hold a moment please." I swept the area looking for any of the soft signs of trouble I might be up to detecting. Like groups of ten or more armed men.

"DeVito here. Glad you called."

"What's happened? I called the Saunders' house and got some guy telling me it was impossible to speak to Mrs. Saunders and to call you."

"Yeah. That was probably the last of the rescue squad guys. Maggie's in Suburban, under sedation. She started to lose it after we dug up Randolph's basement earlier today. I dropped her at her house and she said she'd call her doctor for something to calm her down. By the time he got out there, she was a basket case, so he called to have her admitted to Suburban right away."

"What did you find out there?"

"What didn't we find. Bodies, lot of bodies. Pieces of bodies. In the walls, in the ground—all little ones, man. Tapes—video and sound only. We played the one he used when he called Herb. He had copies of the posters Herb had made up and a tape of Herb's television appeal. It's beyond words. Just incredible. There's a code book too. We don't know what it means, but there're forty-one entries. Forty-one. Going back seven, almost eight years. We think it's got locations, identifying data, God knows what else, all in code. Make my day. Tell me Randolph fell into a Rototiller."

"No such luck at all. I've found Herb Saunders, but I can't get him to go home and let me find Randolph. I was hoping to get Maggie to fly down here to reason with him, but now that's out of the question. By the way, do you know what room she's in?"

"Yeah, three hundred and seventy-four east wing. I'm putting everything I've got on the wires to the police chief down there."

"Anything on Randolph's beach house?"

"Not yet. His papers are all in safe deposit boxes throughout the city. We haven't been able to open them all yet. If I get anything I'll call down there right away." There was a long pause and then DeVito spoke in a voice that was sad, gentle, and tired all at once. "I don't know how you want to use this with Herb, but there ain't much chance those kids are alive. We haven't sorted out all the bodies and there may be ones located elsewhere, but it looks like Randolph killed them all when he was done with them. Maybe Herb'll come home if he knows it's over. Good luck, Haggerty."

"Yeah, thanks." I looked around for some of that on the streets and, like the early signs of trouble, I saw none.

Chapter 20

I RUBBED MY STUBBLY CHIN, TOOK OFF MY GLASSES, AND PRESSED my eyes closed. Things still looked just as bad.

Herb Saunders trotted down the stairs with a wrapped loaf of bread in his hand. He swung around the side of the motel, apparently on his way to the beach. I got back in the car and nosed it into a parking space. Wendy got out as I did. I thought about taking the Remington along with us, but I needed to talk to Saunders and the gun would most likely create more problems than it might solve. I left it guarding the spare tire.

Wendy and I hopped, skipped, and jumped trying to settle into a matching pattern of strides. That done, I looked up and saw Saunders ahead of us. He'd stopped for a moment to take off his shoes and roll up his pants legs. We followed him out the walkway between the dunes to the beach. Spread out all over the sand were gulls, sand pipers, and plovers. Each one stood unmoving, but followed Saunders eyes only as he approached. He stopped at the edge of their congregation, untied the bag of bread, reached in, and flung an offering to them.

All at once the birds were airborne. Hovering, wings flapping in front of Saunders, they snatched out of the air each piece he threw. He moved slowly, easily, calmly with a small smile on his face. He seemed to be enjoying the incessant beating of the wings all around him, the untamed animal energy so close, but without any attendant danger. When his bag seemed close to empty, we walked down toward him. I stood off to the side of him, Wendy beside me. He was still in the eye of the bird storm. The bag was now empty and, just as suddenly as they had arisen, the birds settled back onto the sand, arranged themselves with respect to each other's territory, and ignored us.

Saunders slowly turned to me. I could tell he was angered by our presence. Not wanting to alienate him further, I decided to speak first. "Mr. Saunders, I have some news for you. I've spoken with Pete DeVito. They've been through Randolph's house."

Saunders began to fold the bread wrapper into squares. He alternated between looking down at it to check that each corner was aligned and then back at me. "Yes?"

Here goes nothing. "They found a large number of bodies buried in the house. It seems that whoever he snatched he eventually killed. Pete thought it likely that your girls were in there." There, done.

Saunders stroked his scalp and then gently patted the back of his head. A small gesture of consolation. I remember my father patting me like that once. I'd struck out with the bases loaded. If my bat had been a blade, I'd have fallen on it.

"Have they identified them for sure?" When he finally spoke, his calm startled me.

"No. Not yet."

"Then they might not be there." Though the evidence mounted, he was still hoarding his last scraps of hope.

"If they're not there, then he most likely buried them elsewhere. The man's a killer. He doesn't let people go." I was surprised at my adamance.

"Neither do I, Mr. Haggerty, and I won't let go of my search until I'm absolutely certain they're gone." He began to move back toward the motel.

"There's another piece of news. Your wife is in the hospital, sedated. She apparently broke down when they were bringing the bodies up out of the house. She was asking for you." I pardoned myself for that last lie, hoping it would provide a more compelling mission for him than the one he was on.

Saunders stopped and, withou turning back to me he said, "Is that true, Haggerty?"

I'm a good liar, but I was grateful he wasn't looking me in the eye when I said, "Yeah, it's the truth."

He turned back to me finally and asked, "Where is she?"

"In Suburban, three hundred seventy-four east wing, DeVito said. Why don't you give her a call, talk to her. She needs you." I was starting to chant.

"Yeah. You're right. Hell of a thing to go through alone." Saunders turned back to the motel and strode off. I was dismissed. What did I want, a thanks? I'm just doing a job. I went up to Wendy who had been silent observer to my dealing with Saunders and gave her a report. "I think he might go back home. It looks like his kids have been found . . ."

"Are they okay?" she interrupted, optimistically.

"No. They weren't okay. What they found were bodies." I was starting to feel pretty brutal this afternoon. Announcing deaths like I was running a deli counter: Who's next? How you want it sliced?

"I'm sorry I was so abrupt. I guess I don't know anybody that's okay today and it's getting to me."

"Me too," she said. She turned and walked back to the motel. Standing alone on the beach I felt surprisingly bereft.

I caught up with her at the car. "Look, I'm sorry. What can I say?"

"Nothing. It's okay. I'm just moody. Any little thing can throw me off. When you snapped at me, I just felt all alone again and you were just another man. I'm okay now. What are we going to do?"

I liked the we in that sentence. "Let's go talk to Saunders."

We went back across the parking lot, then up the stairs to Saunders' room. The door was open. He was on the phone with the look of someone on a long hold. On the dresser were two photographs and a homemade Father's Day card. Wendy stepped across the threshold, but stood close by the door. I moved further into the room and stood facing Saunders.

Someone was finally talking to him. He nodded a couple of times and said, "That's okay. Thank you, I'll call back in a while." He cradled the receiver and looked up at me. "She's still under sedation. I'll have to try again."

He got up off the bed and brushed past me to the dresser. He picked up one picture, then the other, and finally he turned back to me. "You're pushing your luck, Haggerty."

"That's what I get paid for. Look—"

"Look nothing. In the old days they killed messengers like you. Maybe it wasn't such a bad idea." He balled his fists.

I put my palms up. "All right. I'm leaving. Call your wife. She needs you."

I backed out of the room as Saunders advanced. When I'd passed through the doorway, Wendy moved to follow me. Before she did, she stopped and turned back to Saunders. "I'm really sorry about your daughters, Mr. Saunders. I can just imagine what you've been through."

Saunders came to a halt. He asked her, "Do your parents know where you are?" The question was utterly devoid of innuendo.

"Yes, they do."

"That's good. I'm glad. We should always know where our loved ones are." Saunders stopped for a moment and looked closely at Wendy's face, searching for a clue, a reason why she was here and his girls weren't.

"How old are you, child?"

"Twenty."

"My girls would be twelve." Saunders' gaze wandered off into memory for a moment then returned to Wendy's face. "You look like a nice person. I'm sure your father loves you very much."

Saunders' eyes glistened, and he took a tottering step toward Wendy. She stiffened and leaned away from him. Her fear and his need were swirling in that room. An emotional storm front was building. I glided toward them slowly. Saunders reached out his hand and gently, feather light, he brushed a stray hair back from Wendy's face. In that touch all his sadness broke loose and formed the words he spoke to her. "I'd give anything in the world to be able to do that to one of my girls. I have a hole in me so big you wouldn't believe, and it just drips blood all the time." His hand fell back to his side and with it the emotional tide crested and receded.

He looked over at me and said, "I'll think about your offer. I need to be alone just now."

"Sure," I said.

Wendy smiled wanly at him, touched his arm once, and then went out the door. Saunders closed it behind us, and we went down the stairs back to the car.

Chapter 21

Sitting in the car, Wendy asked what we were going to do next.

"We wait is what we do next. He wants to be alone now, fine. But he still hasn't changed his plans. So we wait and we watch. This is the exciting stuff the TV detectives do while the commercials are on."

I turned and faced Wendy. "By the way, you were really helpful up there. Thanks."

"I didn't mean to be. I was just telling him how I felt. I meant it."

"I'm sure you did. I just meant that my approach to Saunders wasn't getting us anywhere. What you said unlocked a piece of him I couldn't reach and got us closer to his going home than I thought possible."

"If it was helpful then I'm glad."

Twenty minutes passed before Saunders came down the stairs. At the foot he stopped and looked around, presumably for our car. I got out. Seeing me he walked straight over.

"Haggerty, I've decided to go home. You're right. Maggie needs to be my first concern. I called, but there's no more flights back today. I'll return my rented car tomorrow and catch the afternoon flight back to National."

"She'll be glad to know you're okay. Have you spoken to her yet?"

"No. She's apparently still out. I'll try again later.

"Look, I was going to get something to eat down at one of the waterfront restaurants. Would you care to come along? Frankly I could use the company." The last line was directed through the car window at Wendy, seated inside.

I looked in at her. She said, "Sure."

She got out, and I locked the car. We walked back to the waterfront. I thought us three very weary musketeers. All for one, perhaps, but which one?

All the restaurants were the same. Just as I'd fished up and down the Atlantic Coast, I'd eaten in restaurants like these from Melbourne to Brielle. They were always large bare rooms without style. They existed only as permanently affixed weatherproofed seatings on the ocean's front. The first tables filled were always those right by the floor-to-ceiling wall of glass that ran the entire width of the building. The later you arrived the further back you sat. Your dinner would still have been in the water at noon and that was all to the good. By and large, the cooking was undistinguished. Not bad enough to ruin the fish, but not skilled enough to enhance what the mere freshness of the fish brought to the dish. Portions would be large and the prices low. That fact somehow always added to the quality of the meal. The waitresses were almost always high school girls who were friendly and inefficient.

We were too tired to comparison shop and went into the first one we came to. We were early enough to get a window seating. Our waitress—Tammy, her tag said—left us a bowl of hush puppies, a pitcher of ice water, and three menus. Eventually she found her way back to us and took our orders.

There were too many areas of private pain for conversation to roam freely. Saunders found out that Wendy wasn't my girl friend or secretary, but not how we had come to be together. We talked about the Olympics, the boycott, the upcoming track and field trials, and Wendy's hopes for making the team.

Saunders asked her how she got into throwing the javelin.

"Well, when I was growing up, I played other things. I was always big for my age so I tried basketball and volleyball, and swimming, but I was never very coordinated. So I didn't do too well. I stopped playing them altogether after a while. They're the kinds of games that if you're going to be any good at you have to start early so the skills become second nature to you. Well, I finally got coordinated in high school, but by then it was too late to learn to play those games from scratch.

"I had a boyfriend who threw the shot on the track team so I would go to watch him at practice. I picked up a javelin one day, just fooling around, and he showed me how to throw it. The girls' coach saw me and said I was good enough to make the team. I didn't know she didn't have any javelin throwers at all." Wendy's exuberant laugh brought smiles all around. For a moment it was possible to believe in a world without rape and murder. "Anyway, I turned out to be pretty good, and it was something I wasn't behind in. Nobody else had been throwing javelins in grade school. At least not in America. In Finland I think they put them in the cradles, but what the heck. I just enjoy throwing the thing. The way it makes me feel: for once it's good to be big and strong. Anyway, that's enough about me. Did either of you play anything?" Wendy was blushing ever so slightly.

Saunders said no and I just didn't answer. My attention was on the big man in the cap and sunglasses eating by himself at a table next to the wall. He stared at us too often for chance. Hungerford said Bubba Bascomb would be hard to miss. This guy had good size on him, but sitting down it was hard to tell it he was the giant I was expecting to see. He had soft, pouty lips and a flat nose. His overalls were shapeless, and he was trying his best to fill them with two platters of seafood and a pitcher of beer. All of this was inconclusive. I relaxed when a short, round woman and two equally rotund children came to the table, kissed him on the cheek, and sat down with him. He must have just been having an appetizer.

I looked back and saw Wendy scowling at me. "I'm sorry. I wasn't paying attention. I thought I saw someone staring at us." That got both Saunders' and Wendy's attention. "It wasn't anyone we're looking for. You can relax." They each scanned the room. The spell was broken though, and the grim reasons we were all together had come back to the foreground.

"Let's get the check and leave." I flagged our waitress down and got the check from her. As we wove our way through the incoming crowd, Wendy said she had to go to the bathroom. I asked her to wait until I could stay outside the door. Saunders said he wanted to try and call his wife. Just to let her know he was coming home. I stood in line at the cashier and watched him go off toward the phone booth in the corner. He put in his change, dialed, and then stood there waiting for a connection. He turned around abruptly, and seemed to be looking at two couples seated nearby.

I paid the bill and walked Wendy to the ladies room. As we passed the phone booth I looked over at the table that had drawn Saunders' attention. Neither man matched Randolph's description, but one of the women was the day shift police dispatcher. When I looked back Saunders was speaking animatedly into the phone. He blew a kiss into the receiver and hung up. Wendy came out of the bathroom, and we all left together.

We walked slowly back to the motel. Saunders said, "I think I'll turn in early. I've got to pack up. I've decided to drive back rather than wait for the plane. If I get up early I can be back home by early afternoon."

"Sounds good to me. Think about what I said. If you want, I'll look for Randolph down here for you. Talk it over with your wife. I've got to be down here anyway." I gave Saunders one of my cards. On the back, I scrawled the phone number at Wendy's house.

"Listen, I want to thank you. You were right. It's over. I need to be back with Maggie. Start over. She said to thank you too for finding me and getting me to come home." We shook hands on that.

"Sure. Have a safe trip back." I guided Wendy to the car and watched Saunders mount the steps to his room.

Chapter 22

I GOT IN THE CAR AND AFTER ANOTHER ANTIBOMB INSPECTION, started the engine.

"We've got some shopping to do," I said.

"What?"

"We've got some things to pick up for the night shift."

"What night shift?"

"The one we're about to begin. You've just enrolled in detective school. Tonight's course is Surveillance 101."

"Why?"

"Because if Saunders is going home tomorrow, I'm the tooth fairy. I don't know where he's going, but I expect him to stay put for a few minutes to make sure we're gone. That's why we're going shopping now. To be back in place before Saunders goes anywhere."

We went around the block, and I pulled up in front of a convenience store. Wendy said it was okay to leave her in the car. I left the motor on when I got out and told Wendy to get behind the wheel. If anyone approached the car she was to sit on the horn. If that didn't deter them, she should run them over. I got what we needed in less than five minutes and carried the bag back to the car. I handed it through the window to Wendy and then went to make two phone calls. Nothing that I learned surprised me.

I got back in the car and had Wendy drive us to a spot where we could watch Saunders' motel room.

"Well, what have we got here?" She opened the bag and

took out six large coffees, a $6.99 thermos, a quart jar of apple juice, three sports magazines, and half dozen comic books.

"Pour the coffees into the thermos, Watson." As she did, I opened the door and poured the apple juice out on the ground.

"Why'd you do that?" she asked.

"Because what we need is an empty container, not the apple juice. I leave the reason for that to your imagination."

She frowned for a moment and then laughed.

"Right, Watson. The coffee is to keep us alert. The reading material is to keep us from going bananas. I assumed the magazines would interest you. My apologies if I chose poorly. Don't laugh at the comics. They keep my brain on without being engaged. An interesting book is either wasted or a distraction. These are perfect. If I forget where I am I can always start over without the 'artistic merits' being lost, and they aren't so gripping that I'll forget why I'm really out here in the dark." I handed her the magazines and shoved the comics up on the dashboard. The thermos I put on the floor between us along with the empty jar.

"Make yourself comfortable. We can talk. You can read. Sleep if you can. I'll ask you to spell me after midnight. If you feel like you're fading, wake me right away. Have you got all this? There's going to be a quiz in the morning."

"Sure. No sweat."

"Fine. If the police pull up and ask us what we're doing here, we're having a fight about getting married. I'm having cold feet because you want six kids. Okay?"

"No way. I want to back out because you want six kids."

"Okay. They'll come around for another sweep probably a couple of hours later. Keep an eye out in the mirror for them. As they pull up, let's embrace like we're making up. They love happy endings and will probably pass us by."

"Okay, Sherlock."

"Last thing: any car that goes by real slowly or more than

once or pulls up and parks and no one gets out is trouble. Wake me right away. Got it?"

"Got it."

"Okay. That's the fine points of surveillance."

"Except for one thing. How'd you know Saunders isn't going home?"

"Two things. First, he was just too accommodating. Too willing to just pack up and go home. He didn't say good-bye to you. You got to that man. If he was really calling it quits and leaving, he'd have said good-bye to you. No. It was all a show. Plus I'm a naturally suspicious guy. So I called the hospital. No one's called Mrs. Saunders since this afternoon. She's still sedated. That was all a show for us in the restaurant. Secondly, he was real interested in a conversation that the police dispatcher was having at her table while he was on the phone. I called the police. They wouldn't tell me anything, and Hungerford was out of the office. But I'll bet you dollars to donuts Saunders heard something about Randolph. So we sit and wait. If I'm wrong we can wave bye-bye when he drives off to go home. If I'm right, he may lead us to Randolph."

That night passed like most of them do on surveillance. The silence, darkness, and stillness are a blessed relief at first, especially if you've been busting your chops trying to keep someone in sight all day and remain invisible yourself. You start to relax and unwind. I wished we'd gone back and gotten my car. I spent a fortune putting a custom contoured reclining bucket seat in my car just for times like these. Once you've relaxed, the lack of action begins to be irritating. You ask "why am I here? I should be home sleeping." Custom seat or no, it's not comfortable. You swear you'll up your rates for this crap. The person you're watching is either sleeping better or having more fun than you are. You can't sleep but you're tired, so about then you insert the IV drip of caffeine. More nothing happens. You're bored stupid, tired, uncomfortable, downright cranky. You fire yourself from the case.

The minutes go by so slowly you swear you're watching isolated replays of sloths on parade.

When I was younger, about this time I'd start to sing to myself, tap the steering wheel, look for someone to kill. My partner, Arnie, taught me how to go into a light trance, a hypnoid state of consciousness. Unfocused but easily alerted. So at 3 A.M., I began to imagine my arms and legs were lying off the ends of a soft float, dangling in warm moving water. I slowed my breathing and heart rate. I imagined a stream of water washing through my mind, cleansing me, taking away the grit, the sediment, all thought passing out my fingertips to the sea I imagined I was in.

I looked over at Wendy. After reading her magazine, we had talked for a while. We created fantasy biographies. I was the illegitimate son of Robert Mitchum and Katharine Hepburn. Like most twenty-year-olds, she couldn't imagine a past longer than two weeks ago. I told her she was the whispered-about legendary child of Joe DiMaggio and Marilyn Monroe.

She dug a Walkman out from the glove compartment, plugged herself in, and mercifully fell asleep. In my waking dream state she was lovely. She turned sideways with her legs curled up. Her head lay against the seat back with her hands for a pillow. I watched the rhythmic rise and fall of her chest. She slept without incident. I was glad for her.

I watched the night sky absorb the rays of the coming sun until daybreak. First, light leaked and then streamed through the saturated sky. As the giant orange ball burned off the cloud cover, Herb Saunders came down the motel stairs. He stopped and looked carefully both ways before crossing. Then he walked quickly down the street away from us. He was carrying a black bag.

Chapter 23

TONY MAGLIOTTI WAS MISSING. HE HADN'T COME HOME FROM school. His parents called everywhere. No one had any ideas. Tony was a good boy. He always went straight home. They called his friends, the Bible class teacher, the hospital. Nothing. Finally they had come to see their priest. Waiting for them he felt formless, leaden.

His assistant told him they had arrived. He couldn't get up to take a step. He was paralyzed. They'll just have to go home, he thought. He'd have Cecilia tell them. Slowly his resolve reasserted itself. *My mind is just running away with me. I'll put my hands on my knees and up we go. Simple. Now one foot in front of the other. See, walking. Open the door. Our father who art in heaven . . .*

They were in his study. "Mr. and Mrs. Magliotti. Please sit down. How can I help you in this terrible time?" He already knew the answer. He could tell them who had their child and why.

"We got a phone call just a little bit ago. A man said come see you. That you knew where Tony was. Well, what did he mean?"

"I'm sorry, I don't know. I don't know where Tony is. I don't know why someone would say such thing."

"Yeah. That's a good question. Why? He told us why. He said there's a killer here in our town. A child killer and he's got Tony. That he's seen you in confession and you know who he is. Is that true?"

Mr. Magliotti was on his feet, vibrating with rage. His wife was shredding a tissue and looking back and forth at the men like a manic metronome. "So, so tell me. Is this true, huh?"

Oh God. Yea, though I walk through the valley . . . "Yes, it's true." At first the priest couldn't look at him, then slowly he did.

"How could you do this? How could you do this? It's Tony. He sings for you. He wants to grow up and be just like Father Gus. This is no newspaper story. He's one of ours. It's my son. Tell me. Tell me, God damn you."

He jerked the priest back and forth. In his fury, he was tearing off the lapels of his coat.

"I cannot. It's sacred. Anything I know from the confessional is sacred. I can't. I can't. I can't." Father Shannon waved his arms, but Magliotti was not a dream. He didn't go away. Father Shannon kept swatting until he freed himself.

"Listen, we'll keep it a secret. No one needs to know. It'll be just between us. I swear to you. I promise. So help me God. Just tell us where the man is, what he looks like." Magliotti's hands were open now in entreaty, asking the priest to intercede for them. It was in his power.

"I can not. God forbids it. It is my duty as a priest. I wish I could. Lord knows. But I cannot break that vow. You are Catholics. You know that." He hoped they did or would at least tell him so.

"So it's your duty. Who says you've got to be perfect. You can't slip, make a mistake, sin, and repent. Don't you teach he's a God of mercy? He'll forgive you. Look what's at stake here. A life, a human life. A one-time gift from God. When it's gone, it's gone. You don't think your precious duty could recover a little easier. Tell me that, priest. Are you so much a man of God that you're no longer a man of the people?"

Father Shannon was tired. He wanted to answer him. He understood his feelings. He also felt he shouldn't be burdened with understanding him. Though we all live our lives in God's drama, the plot is not revealed. He could only play his part as his heart and whole being told him to. He prayed Tony would be found. How would he live with it if he wasn't? He scourged himself: a duty to uphold can be laid down. It was a choice: his faith or a life, perhaps. Was he that selfish, that narcissistic, was his faith all important? No. An easy faith is no faith, a comfortable faith is no faith. You can't don it like a smoking jacket and then shuck it when it binds. This is God's will, God's way. I am his instrument, He alone is my judge. He who asks much of us, so very much of us as He did of his own only begotten son.

Father Shannon had found his knees. "Help me, Father, to be strong enough in this time of need, to submit to your will, to know that in the end, each act of faith hastens the return of Jesus, our savior. To believe that the good and the innocent, Tony Magliotti perhaps, will at that time and forever more sit in perfect bliss and harmony at your side. To remember that these tests are bitter, the pain so real, because only love of such strength as to endure them forges the bonds for your eternal domain.

"It must be 'I cannot go farther' not 'I will not.' If I fall, it must be from exhaustion at trying to stay upright, not from finding the bow a better posture for a while. I can not choose to sin. I may be weak. I may fall. I may ask for his mercy and strength to help me rise up. But I can not do it on purpose as a sham. I cannot demand forgiveness because it was just too hard back there. I would be using God to ease my burdens, to accept less."

Magliotti stared at him, enraged, horrified perhaps. He grabbed his wife. "You'll answer for this. I swear it. Somewhere: to the law, to the Church. I won't let this rest. This won't go away, Mr. Shannon. Everyone will know. I'll spread it all over town. You'll answer for this, you better believe it."

"Oh, I know, Mr. Magliotti, I will answer someday for

this as I will for all the deeds of my life, and until then, I'll question this every day I have left."

Magliotti grabbed his wife and hauled her to her feet. "C'mon, let's go." As she stumbled out behind him, a black clad reluctant pull-toy, she turned back, "Pray for us, Father. Pray for all of us."

Chapter 24

HERB SAUNDERS WATCHED THEM LEAVE. IT HAD BEEN QUITE a break hearing that lady cop talking in the restaurant. He knew beyond a doubt that Randolph was here and he'd done his work. The priest would soon know that Randolph was the rock and he the hard, hard place. He muttered to himself, "You wanted a test of faith. Okay, I'll give you a test of faith. I told you, get between me and my girls at your own peril. There's nothing I wouldn't do. That was no threat."

Father Shannon stumbled out of the church. Saunders could see he'd had a rough go of it. Saunders prayed silently: You can save a life here. You won't talk *about* him, but you could go talk *to* him. As the priest began to cross the street, he silently cheered him on. *That's it, look both ways, c'mon. Find him for me. Bring him to me. Come to papa. C'mon. Do it, do it, damn you. All right. Let's go. I'm coming girls."*

Chapter 25

We were on the end of a caravan. An ecumenical pilgrimage to a most unholy shrine, Justin Randolph's home, I guessed. Up ahead, a priest was leading the way. Behind him, a supplicant in search of justice. At the end of the line were the two witnesses. That's the purest heroism left for late twentieth century man. To witness and then to testify. Anything more decisive seems to have the stature of a lesser evil. So far, that's been good enough for me.

The priest was the missing link. I knew Saunders. Saunders knew him. Unless there were more links to the chain he knew Justin Randolph. An unlikely pairing.

There was a palpable intensity to the procession. The priest never looked about him, only straight ahead at the house at the end of the block. Saunders only had eyes for the priest. I felt myself dragged along in that magnetic field, knowing that something awful was waiting for us in that house. As it became clear there was only one place we could be going, I sheared off from the procession and jogged with Wendy down a parallel alley that would bring us up alongside the house. There we waited. I looked around the house. There was a back porch and deck. Across the alleyway was an apparently abandoned dry dock office. Beyond that, a small stand of concrete blockhouses painted a mushroom color and entitled U-Rent-A-Locker.

The priest was coming up to the house. He stopped and walked around to the car in the driveway. After looking in the windows, he tried to open the doors. They were locked. The front door opened. From my position, I could hear but not see Randolph. The priest looked up at him, then bounded up the stairs, shouting "Where is he? What have you done with him? Answer me!" All he got in reply was laughter.

The front door slammed twice. Saunders was on his way up the stairs. Things were going to get wild real soon. I turned to Wendy, "Stay right here. Don't move. I'm going to try to go in the back way and keep Saunders and Randolph apart. If I don't come out and tell you it's okay in five minutes, run back to the car, right down the middle of the street yelling fire at the top of your lungs. Go to the nearest phone you can find and call Hungerford."

"Okay, I will." She slipped a brief smile into my memory. I held it there like a good luck charm.

I crouched, crab-walked down the alley's low retaining wall, and then vaulted it into the backyard. The front door slammed one more time. Now playing: Murder in the Cathedral. I loped up the back stairs and flattened myself against the wall. Slowly, I peeked around the window frame. Randolph had a gun in his hand. He waved it back and forth between Saunders and the priest.

The priest was livid. "Where is he? What did you do to him? I beg you, return him. I never revealed your secret. Why do this?"

Randolph laughed, "You fool. You pathetic simpleton. You still don't know what this is about. You're a carrier, a messenger like all the rest. And the message is 'death to you all.'" Randolph snarled as he spoke. Saunders' face was placid. He'd found what he was looking for and it was everything he'd hoped it would be. I watched his hand move in the black bag that dangled from his wrist. "My tale to you would have been meaningless without a death for you to be responsible for. Yes, keep the secret by all means, take it to your grave, rot with it. That's what I intended for you to do.

"Live long, priest. Scourge yourself every day. You can't kill yourself and you can't share it. What an exquisite gift. A life ruined and inescapable. Any way out of this life costs you heaven. What a creation. Oh, you're my crowning achievement, Father. What a burden you take for yourself. 'Lamb of God, accept our sins and cleanse the world!' Okay, you've accepted my sins, now live with them." Randolph shook his head and sneered. He was delighted with himself.

"Unfortunately, you've dragged this gentleman into things and complicated what was to be a vacation for me. Now I'll have to kill you both. Fortunately for you, due to time constraints, I will have to settle for mere efficiency in doing you."

The priest was open mouthed, horrified, brain blasted, as if he'd just found himself on Golgotha when Jesus asked his Father to explain Himself.

Saunders spoke softly, but without fear to Randolph as if he didn't want to provoke him to flight. "Just one question before we proceed. You took my daughters from me. I want to know what you did with them."

Randolph smiled. "You must be kidding. Why should I tell you anything? You'll be dead soon enough. What difference will it make?"

"I need to know. I need to rest, to sleep. Even if it's just for a moment before I die."

"Mercy's not my department. Although if you begged and amused me, I might relent." Randolph was enjoying every minute of this.

The priest knelt and did the begging for Saunders. "For God's sake man, I beg you, tell him where his children are."

Randolph howled. "Always the preface, the anchor for your sheep: for God's sake, always His will. It's always so clear. Well, you've done your part straight down the line and look where you are. Where's your God now? I'm your god. The beginning and end."

"Bullshit." The ferocity in Saunders' voice startled Randolph.

He was drawn, fascinated, to the man who, without hope or reason still defied him. "You're a monster, Randolph. You love to hurt people and destroy things, plain and simple. All the rest is bullshit. There's a God, and I fully intend to assist you in meeting Him." Saunders began to pull something from his bag. The priest leaped on Randolph's gun. I pulled back the screen door when the scream cut the air like a scythe and drew everyone's eyes.

"Leo. Leo. Help me!"

I ran to the end of the deck. Wendy was gone. God damn. I'd been too damn interested in following Saunders and paid too little attention to our being followed. Damn it. I vaulted off the deck and went back down the alley. The front door to the dry dock was open.

"C'mon in, Haggerty."

I focused on the voice: cocky, very cocky. Didn't even bother with surprise. I stepped into the shadows. My eyes adjusted, picking up shades, forms, details. The slag heap on the desk spoke, "Made you a promise, city boy. You really shoulda took me up on that. Avoided a lot of trouble. Just forgot about it.

"But you didn't. I'm a-bettin' you got some damn fool idea 'bout being a hero to this girl." He shook his head to a corner where I could pick out Wendy frozen in the corner, clutching her purse to her chest and DuWayne holding her by a fistful of hair with his one good arm.

"Now I'm sure if she didn't think you were gonna protect her she'd know what to do. Get real forgetful like. I'm bettin' you're behind all this trouble. You're what's keepin' her memory sharp. So's I'm gonna show her how wrong she is. I'm gonna do such a hurt dance on you so's you nevuh forget me." He turned to his brother. "Bring that bitch up here. Let her see what happens to people who make trouble."

"What's in it for you, Bubba? You've got no stake in this."

"Hell. He's family. Don't matter what he done. He's family."

DuWayne dragged Wendy up to the desk Bubba sat on. "Lemme see what got you in so much trouble." Bubba turned and took her face in his hands. He tried to eat her face. She cringed but couldn't pull away.

Carelessly, Bubba squeezed her breast. "Not bad. Might take a piece of you when this is all over, honey."

Wendy shrank back and spit in his face. I never saw him hit her, but she crashed into the wall and slid down it like a raindrop into a puddle on the floor. She wasn't out, but definitely dazed.

Bubba heaved himself off the desk. "Watch closely, DuWayne. You might learn something. I ain't put a major league whipping on a man in a long time. The work'll do me some good."

"What are you gonna do, talk me to death? If you want to dance, start the music."

When he got up, I got the bad news: Big Bubba no blubber. I took a deep breath. I knew I'd seen bigger men, but they were all made of marble. He balled up his fists and came straight at me. I moved out into the center of the floor. Bubba's moon face had thin cornsilk hair and washed-out blue eyes. There was a mild sunburn on his heavy arms. Slope-shouldered and barrel-chested, he had bird legs and he moved well on them.

Coming forward, he was leaning. A tad top heavy. He smiled. The man was having a party, a regular ball. With big men you've got to be coy, staying just out reach. Don't let them get you into close quarters where their strength and size pay off. And you have to be patient. Wear 'em down, not tear 'em down. Then you cut them up a little bit at a time, into bite-size pieces. Or so the theory goes.

I danced in front of him, bobbing, weaving my hands up high to protect my head. I kept my mouth shut, not baiting him. He didn't need any more adrenaline in his mix. I wanted him to work for me. It doesn't matter how big the body unless the engine can move it. Heart and lungs: carburetor and pistons, oxygen and blood — fuel mix. They work just as hard swinging and missing as hitting. I wanted to work him and stay in one piece until he started to stall out, misfire — then make him pay.

I stole a glance around the room. Wendy was propped up against the wall shaking her head. DuWayne sat mesmerized on the desk like he was watching a schoolyard fight with big brother. Bubba threw a right at my head that I just slipped and circled away from. The draft from the blow almost unlaced my shoes. I fired a right jab at his nose. It flowered on his face. Let him suck a little of his own blood for once. I moved away again. He sniffled and came at me lunging and threw a long overhand right barely missing me again. Lord, let me be quick, 'cause if he ever connects I'm gonna be dead on arrival.

I moved in a circle, Bubba lunging past me off balance. His flank was an inviting as a butcher's chart. I went for kidney, but got short ribs instead. My hand was okay. Bubba spun on me, his eyes slits, his teeth bared.

I set up again, eyeing him for fatigue. No such luck. It takes a well-tuned engine to move that big a frame. Bubba looked fine. I could sense DuWayne behind me. He'd have to go sooner or later. I spun and slashed my hand across his throat, knife edge to larynx, crushing it. DuWayne clutched at his throat and toppled backward over the desk. Crouching, I spun through to face Bubba. He had brought both hands thudding down on the desk. "DuWayne, DuWayne, you okay? Talk to me." DuWayne was drumming his heels on the floor and whooping like an asthmatic in a poodle parlor. I snap-kicked Bubba's left knee. It buckled. A backhand lashed out high on my head. I hit the wall. Move. Move. I rolled away and got to my feet. I began to circle Bubba again. He cut off the distance. Bubba's alligator brain was starting to work. I was in trouble.

I wasn't sure I could hurt him enough to back him up. His hands were open and poised before him like a forklift. I got to a crouch. I wasn't about to tie up with him. He charged. I put my right hand on the floor between us and scythed my left arm in a circle, snapping my body behind it as Bubba went by, going for the single leg sweep. I hooked his ankle, but went too far past, rolling over on my side. I held on to the ankle and pulled it to my chest. Bubba was on his back, but so was I. His boot loomed above my face, and I saw the razor in his heel. I rolled back to the left as he boot cracked down. We scrambled to out feet and circled each other.

Bubba was starting to suck wind, to breathe through his mouth. His head wobbled on its perch. His engine was starting to shut down. Soon, he'd come to a grinding halt, all of his muscles twitching and misfiring in spasms. Like a toy soldier running down, the hands weren't held so high. The gap between the will and its acts grew ever greater. Reflexes would soon halt. I hoped I'd be there to kick his tires.

I snuck a glance at Wendy. She was up, braced against the wall, fumbling with her purse. "Get out. Get out now." She was wobbly. I wasn't even sure she heard me.

Bubba took a deep breath and got low. I circled again. He favored the leg I'd kicked in, but I hadn't ruined it for him. He fired out. I tried to read his charge, but he leaped into the air. Too fast. Too fast. Bubba was on me. We fell backward. I tried to knee him, but without force. I pulled my chin down as I felt Bubba's hands on my throat. I slammed my arms against his, but he had three hundred pounds braced on them like pilings for a pier. He kept his head at a safe distance so I couldn't butt him, his chin down protecting his own throat. I spread my arms out, cupped my palms, and slammed them against his ears, driving spikes of air through his eardrums. He howled. His grip loosened, but he didn't let go. I reached for his left arm and grabbed his thumb, peeling it backward to his wrist like a banana. He howled again. I rolled out from under him. Our eyes locked. Get up, get up. He's too close, too close. I crabbed away trying to loosen my throat like it was a tie. Bubba shambled in front of me, swinging the arm with the useless hand.

I got to my feet, but my legs were dead. No movement. Bubba was on me like a wave. I was up in the air. He had me in a bear hug, crushing my ribs. I couldn't breathe. I flailed like a beetle on its back. Head. Head. Kill the head. I butted him. Nothing. Too close to punch. Eyes. Eyes. Blind him. Bubba butted me back and buried his head on my chest. Sparks erupted. I was cut loose. Floating. Shrinking to a point. Period. The end. Too much dog. Too much dog. Sorry.

Bubba screamed. I fell away like dirty laundry. Each breath a gasp, I fought up to my knees. Bubba was roaring, clawing the air. He started to stagger, then to moan. He turned away from me. Wendy was draped limply across his back, both hands locked around the handle of the biggest knife in the house, sunk into him like a harpoon. Bubba crashed to the floor. I couldn't stand upright, but I went to Wendy and pried her hands off the handle and pulled the blade free. Her eyes were riveted shut. I pulled her to her feet and, arms around each other, we staggered out to the street.

"Listen. You did it. You did it. Goddamn. You did it. Oh, God. I thought I was dead." I hugged her to me, so tight it hurt. Right then I loved her. I loved being alive. I held on to her for dear life. I could feel her return the pressure, her fingers clutching the fabric of my shirt. I tried to take my first deep breath and inhaled her scent. Sweet life. I squeezed her once again and whispered in her ear, "Listen, go across the street to find a phone and get Hungerford over here, understand? Tell him what happened and that Saunders went down to the house at the end of the block. That's where I'm going. Got it?"

She nodded against my chest. I looked into that face and

my impeccably reasoned restraint vanished. I could care less about recapturing my past. It was my present and its descendants I wanted to celebrate. I wanted to kiss her with enough passion to taste it still on my deathbed. We gave it our best shot.

I let go of her and we went our separate ways.

Chapter 26

I WALKED AS BRISKLY AS MY RIBS WOULD LET ME BACK TO THE
house. The front door was open. I started up the stairs, but
stopped when I saw the open car trunk. I went back down
the stairs to the car sick from thinking about what would be
there. A boy was folded up in it. He'd been spindled and
mutilated too. I went back up the stairs. It felt like I was
slogging through quicksand. From the start, I'd been too late
and I was getting farther behind by the minute.

The priest was lying facedown on the floor. I knelt next
to him, got my hands under his arms, and turned him over.
He was dead too. Judging from the wounds, he'd grabbed
the gun and pressed it against himself. The bullet had torn
through his right hand and then blasted away his chest. I got
up and went through the silent house. My mind spun like
an emergency flasher with instants of red rage, blue despair,
and yellow caution. I hoped and feared that I'd find more
bodies. A quick but careful search of the house found nothing.

I went out on the deck and looked up and down the beach
and over at the nearby docks. Where the hell would Saunders
go? Randolph would have gone in his car if he could. No.
Saunders had him. Otherwise the trunk would have been
closed. He'd want to be alone with him as he'd said, free
from intrusions. A room somewhere? Not his motel room.
A place he could go to any time he wanted. He couldn't tell
when he'd find Randolph. Any time he wanted. Just call me

first. The bandy-legged waterman. A boat. I ran for the dock.

Down the street and through the gate I sprinted, feeling each and every step. At the far end a boat was making ready to depart. Saunders was bent over, tossing off the lines. I ran down the dock. Randolph was nowhere in sight. The boat was pulling away. Oh shit. I jumped for it. Made it. The boat pitched and gave way. I lurched across the deck and grabbed the rigging to one of the booms to keep from going over. Turning I yelled to Saunders, "Don't do this . . ." I got the rest I so badly needed from the butt of a gaffing hook. The deck was moving and I couldn't catch up with it. I tried. I fought to a slump and rested against the railing.

When I came to, Saunders had his back to me. He was stooped over, working at something with his hands. He stepped back and I saw his handiwork: Justin Randolph on his knees and naked, his hands tied behind his back, with a hawser under his armpits. Saunders was moving around him checking the knots like he was going to get a merit badge for all this. Then he got up and disappeared below deck. When he returned, he had his black bag, an ice chest, and a large metal bucket. Saunders sat down on the deck hatch, reached in and pulled a large serrated knife from his bag. Randolph was on his knees facing him. Saunders pulled a fish from the ice chest by the tail and slammed its head on the hatch cover, stunning it. He cut off its head with a slow sawing motion. Then he turned it belly up, rammed the blade into it, and slit it from gills to tail. Peeling back the meat, he pulled the guts out with his hand.

Saunders stood up, walked up over to Randolph, and smeared the blood and guts all over his chest. I felt like I was watching an Aztec sacrifice, only this wasn't PBS. Saunders repeated the process with enough fish to fill the metal bucket. After gutting them, he chopped them into chunks. Some he smeared on Randolph, some he didn't. He rubbed the blood into Randolph's hair, arms, and back and finally pressed his bloodstained hands on Randolph's face. I knew what he was doing, but asked anyway, hoping that I was wrong.

He got up and sat in one of the fighting chairs, pulled out a cigarette, cupped his hands around the flame, and looked at me. "I don't know what I'm doing, Haggerty. That depends on our friend here, Mr. Randolph. Right now you could say I'm preparing a stew. Mr. Randolph is the main ingredient. Call it shark fin soup, perhaps. Whether dinner is served and who eats whom is up to our guest."

"But why? It's pretty clear he killed your kids. The search is over. Let the law have him. Go home to Maggie."

"It's not that simple, Haggerty. I don't know exactly what I want to do. I need to sort that out. I've spent four years waiting for this moment: when I find out where my girls are and what happened to them. There'd be a cleansing in that knowledge. I'd know finally one way or another. I'd force it out of him. Instead, it seems to have just washed over me: what you said DeVito told you, what he said to the priest. I feel like I know. They're dead, and I got no satisfaction out of tearing that secret out of him. I don't know what I'm going to do."

With that, he got up, went into the cabin, and returned with a large ladle. He sat on the stern and spooned the chum behind the boat. I looked at the sky. It was overcast, and in the distance dark storm clouds were gathering. The wind was coming up. This was not the time to be calling all sharks.

Randolph followed Saunders with his eyes. "Perhaps they're not dead. I might have let them live. They were very beautiful. Twins. I remember them well."

Saunders whirled. "Shut up, you scumbag. Don't you talk about my girls. Yes, they were beautiful. They were innocent and kind and loving. And you destroyed that. And for that you'll pay, you son of a bitch."

Randolph went on anyway. His voice was thin with desperation. "Can you really afford not to believe me? No one knows what really happened but me. Return me to shore, and I'll tell you if they're alive or not and where they are."

"Never. No deals. You'll talk or die."

"Don't be ridiculous. We need only trade. Give me what I want and I'll give you what you want."

I broke in. "Saunders, don't buy into this shit. DeVito searched his house. There was a code book with entries for everything. When they crack it, they'll know what happened to your girls." I snuck a glance at Randolph. His wide-eyed stare convinced me the answers were in that book. "Look at him, It's true. Look at him."

Saunders turned back and was convinced by what he saw. He backhanded Randolph in the face, knocking him over on his side. I was afraid Randolph's lifespan was down to minutes.

"Turn him over to DeVito. Let the law have him."

"What will they do to him? Huh? He'll plead insanity, childhood trauma, get some lawyer who thinks that 'due process' is holy, fuck the outcome. I was just doing my duty — providing the best defense.' Hell, we laughed at that at Nuremberg. No way. He'll wind up getting sent to some hospital where he'll snow the fools there and be on the streets before we are."

"I am not insane. That would demean me. I am not a failure, the product of some familial defect. I am a free man. Free of the petty restraints of you sheep. I am different, better . . ." Randolph was struggling to right himself.

Saunders went over and pulled Randolph's face up to his by the hair. Their eyes locked. They were close enough to breathe the same air. "Damn right you're not insane. Not in my book, motherfucker. I don't give a damn what happened to you growing up or what made you what you are. Somewhere along the way you knew you were doing wrong because you kept it a secret. And you went on and on. Over and over you did wrong, and you did nothing to stop yourself. Let the others pay the price, not you. Well, I'm here to collect. You're way past due, motherfucker."

We were starting to get a fair chop to the waves, which was keeping me slightly nauseated. I wasn't about to risk jumping Saunders until my head stopped spinning and my legs firmed up. Instead, I hoped to halt him with words, give him enough decisions to make, enough outcomes to balance to freeze his brain.

"Saunders, don't do this. Can't you see you're giving him just what he wants?"

"He wants to die?" Saunders arched his eyebrows quizzically.

"No. But he wants the stink of his handiwork to live after him. That's why he used that priest. Think about it. Each death is just the beginning. He wants the rage and guilt to persist and to poison the lives of everyone else. Look at you: four years consumed by this obsession. He got you. It worked. Free yourself. Set it aside. Even if you kill him, your girls won't come back. Your grief won't end. But the rest of his control of you will. Without the survivors carrying his curse, the memory of him inside, he dies. He's nothing, nothing. Remember your girls, not him."

Randolph was becoming more agitated as I spoke. Finally he shrieked at us. "Can you forget me? No, you can't escape me. I'll haunt you forever. Your life is mine. Can you close your eyes and not imagine what I did to them? Those soft little bodies. Try to forget this: On the first day I—"

Saunders was on him in a fury. His hands were around his throat. "Shut up, you animal. Shut up." Randolph's face mottled. He gasped for air. Suddenly Saunders hoisted him overhead and in one titanic heave, threw him overboard. "Die, you son of a bitch, die."

I'd missed my chance. I lifted myself up the rigging. "Think, man. Bring him in. We'll gag him. Shut him up. Don't you think the rest of his life in a prison would punish him enough? Who would he hurt there or control? He'll be a victim the rest of his life."

"But he'd still have the sun and cool breezes. The special decency of a Christmas dinner. Television. Books to read. He'd have a life. Not much, but a life. My girls have none, so neither will he. Now sit down, Haggerty. I have a job to finish." With that he pulled Randolph's pistol from under his shirt.

I watched him ladle the chum over the side of the boat. He cut some of the chunks into smaller pieces. When he was done he tossed the knife back into his bag. He looked up at the sky, "Good. There's a storm coming. The turbulence will bring them up from the bottom. Out here we'll get the big ones, the ocean cruisers."

Randolph was bug-eyed, looking all around him, pedaling a liquid bicycle, gulping and spitting water. Saunders yelled to him, "Good. Thrash. You're a dinner bell. They're coming for you, Randolph. They're down there. You're food, Randolph. Dinner's served." Saunders braced himself on the edge of the railing, looking for the first fins.

"What are you going to do with me, Saunders? Kill me too? Then there's no one out here to tell what happened. A fishing accident, perhaps. You'll go home and lie down next to Maggie. What will you tell her about the detective she hired to find you? Is it getting that easy to kill, Herb?"

"Shut up, damn you. I've done all my killing. I don't care who you tell. It's over."

"Is it? You'll go to jail, Herb. Maggie'll have nothing, nothing. Think about that. Think hard because you're running out of time." The first fin had broken the water.

Randolph shrieked, "Something's here. It touched me. Bring me in. God, bring me in. I'm begging you."

"Maggie needs you. She told me so. Without someone to

care for she'd have died. Killed herself she said. Think about it. Up there alone, she collapsed. She needs you. She loves you. I hear she carried you, man, for years. So you're going to throw that away for this piece of shit. She really must have wasted her fucking time, taking care of you. For what? Did you ever love her? Can you remember her? Think about her — that's what you're throwing away, that woman and all she did for you, for this."

I searched the sea for Randolph. He was gone. Then he appeared. The crest of the waves was blocking him from view. He was gone again. I heard a shrill yipping sound. "A-y-a-y-ee! It's here. Oh God. Bring me in!"

Saunders looked at me. All his energy was gone. He was unplugged, almost inert. "You're right. Let's go."

I patted his back and hobbled to the railing. Hand over hand I began to reel Randolph in. Saunders had cleated the line and was moving to the wheel to bring the boat around.

An enormous crack, like a shot, seemed to fill the world. We were inside a sound. The boat rocked, then tilted. I grabbed the rigging. For a second, I thought we'd keel over. Saunders had been flung across the cabin. The galleyway hatch had hit him in the forehead and like a marionette he folded up and sat down. The boat leveled out.

I went back to the railing to look for Randolph. First I saw the gray shape that had smacked us with its tail. He was sixteen feet if he was an inch and probably weighed close to a ton. It was sliding alongside us between the boat and Randolph. The chum had attracted it and, confused by the turbulence of the propellers, it thought we were a giant wounded seal. It gave us a whack to be sure we were dead and was now waiting to see what we'd do.

I uncleated the line to Randolph, ran it around the stern to the other side of the boat and reaffixed it. Saunders I hauled down to a bunk, grabbed a line, and tied him into it. He was still out cold. In this chop and with our current companions

I didn't want Saunders coming to and lurching groggily across the deck into the sea. I took the wheel and spun it hard trying to keep the boat between Randolph and the shark. I looped a line over the wheel and tied it in place. The chum bucket was still half full. I reached in for the biggest chunks and threw them into the water as far from the boat and Randolph as I could. The fin had disappeared. I took the whole bucket and threw it in that direction. I crossed the deck and looked for Randolph as I began to pull in the line. I saw him. "Randolph, listen to me. If anything bumps you, kick it hard. Sharks want easy prey. If you fight back, you aren't worth the trouble." I kept pulling him in, eyeing the water for dark shapes moving under the surface. I kept pulling: one, two, one, two. Randolph was getting closer. I didn't know how I'd hoist him up. I kept pulling. He was about six feet away off the port side.

"Hurry, please. Help me." He was pleading.

I bent down, looking for a gaffing hook to pull him in with. Randolph's shriek cleaved me in two. I snapped upright. Randolph was right next to me rising out of the water, up to his waist in a shark's mouth. It was tail-walking away from the boat, gulping him down. Randolph's arms were pinned behind him, hooked over the shark's snout. I was petrified. Our eyes met once. His were past terror, sending a momentary plea that I answered with a useless reflex extension of my hand. Then, they simply recorded his last sights as he slid silently below the surface.

I stood there stunned. A terrific blow snapped across my back pitching me forward, pinning me to the rail. The rope. The rope to Randolph. The shark was dragging him out to sea and pinning me to the side. My left leg jerked up. I was on my back. What the hell—? A loop. I was hooked in the rope. I tried to kick free. Another snap rammed me against the hull. I couldn't move the leg. It was going numb. If I didn't go over, it would be cut off right here.

Another tug. I was running out of rope. One more and I'd be hoisted right over. Oh, Jesus. I was upside down. I slid into something. Saunders' bag. I pulled it over onto it's side. The knife clattered out. I reached for it, grabbed the blade and finger walked along it back to the handle. Gripping it I bent forward and began to saw at the lines. Oh God, give me a fuckin' break. I sawed, I slashed. My teeth were gritted. I squinted. The inexorable tempo of breath, in and out, was suspended in one last effort: interlude or eternity. I awaited one last tug. Through. I rolled away. The line danced up like a cobra, slapped a good-bye against the rigging, and was gone.

I lay on the deck, gasping, slowly coming back to life. My fingers were clenched around the knife. I unlocked them, took a deep breath, then another. Breathe and wince. Breathe and wince. I massaged my leg, wiggled my foot, slowly felt all my joints. Moved myself in pieces, tuning up before the first symphonic movement: standing up. That done, I creaked across the deck to the cockpit and picked up the radio mike. I flipped the On switch. "Hello, hello. Anybody out there? This is the . . ." What the fuck. I didn't know the boat's name. I looked around. It was block lettered on the captain's log. *"Tommy's Pride 'n Joy.* We're lost. Hello, hello. Can anybody hear me?" I twisted the dial trying to get anyone else's messages. Nothing. I craned my neck out of the cabin. In the distance the storm clouds were purple over gray. Lightning dove at the ground. There was now plenty of static. I doubted anyone could hear us. "Hello, hello. Mayday. We're lost. Anybody out there? Mayday, mayday. Help. We're lost. We're lost. Anybody there? Anybody at all. Can you hear me?"

I looked at the charts and the compass. Christ, I was a detective, not a boat captain. I had no idea what I was looking at. I spread the maps out, looked at the depth readings and the coastline. Without any idea where I was, a heading was impossible to figure. My first goal was to stay afloat and keep calling for help. The sea was still rising and the wind was up. Rain began to pelt the boat. I battened down the hatches, took down the riggings, and made sure the booms were locked in. Saunders was still out, but breathing regularly. After rummaging around for a couple of minutes, I found another line. Having knotted it around my waist, I tied myself to the wheel. There'd be no rescue until the storm passed.

My only goal was not to capsize and to that end I steered a course with the waves throughout the night. I stood at the radio and talked into the silent mike for hours. Even under the cockpit the rain got in and I was soaked to the bone. I swear the sun didn't come up the next day. It just kept raining and blowing. Early on that second day panic approached me and made an offer. After serious negotiation I was able to convince myself that if we stayed afloat and rode out the storm, we'd be rescued. People knew the boat was gone. There was a big coast guard base nearby. If after the storm broke we weren't picked up I was going to take that real bad. I could feel both a huff and a snit coming.

The cramps hit me later that day. First my legs went. I lay down on the deck, mike in hand talking to myself. Then my guts knotted up. I tried to puke but had nothing to give up. So I just cramped and spasmed and rode them out. They began to harmonize with the sound of the waves hitting the boat. I looked at the wheel, it was spinning freely now. I was too tired to give a damn. I was grateful for that. I spent forever listening to the sea's dull slap against the side. At some point, I thought it merged into the *thwop thwop* of helicopter blades, but it wasn't until I awoke in Wendy's smile that I was sure.

Chapter 27

THAT SMILE, WHICH WARMED ME CLEAR THROUGH, WAS ADMINistered in the county hospital. I could tell because I try never to see my clients with an IV running.

"Hi there," I said feebly.

"Hi there yourself. God, it's good to have you back. You've been out of it for a while." She squeezed my free hand.

"It's good to be back. Last thing I remember was wanting to be buried at sea. What happened?"

"There was a storm. I guess you know that. You rode it out. That was Saturday and Sunday. Today's Monday. I called Chief Hungerford. They figured out when that boat didn't come in that you all were on it. Nobody could go out until it cleared." She took a deep breath. "Let me tell you, you had me scared when they brought you in. You were blue. I swear it. And you had these attacks that just shook you from head to foot, like waves or something going through you. When they took you into emergency, I asked the doctor afterward how you were. He said you were hypothermic and dehydrated and had these cramps because your electrolytes or something were all out of wack. You just needed to be kept warm and quiet. You slept for fourteen hours. And, oh yeah, this stuff," she tapped the lines, "it's supposed to straighten out all your imbalances."

"Great. Tastes like hell though." I wiggled the hand the IV ran into.

"How's Saunders? Did he make it?"

"Yeah. He had a concussion. He's in the next room. His wife and a police officer—DeVito I think—are here with him. Lots of people have shown up. My folks are here. They said when you get out of here you can rest up in the extra room at the house."

"Tell them thanks. I wouldn't stay anywhere else. How about you?" I tried to squeeze her hand back.

"Oh, okay, I guess. The trials are out though." She held up her right arm in a soft cast.

"What happened?"

"When that guy, Bubba, hit me and I hit the wall I chipped a bone in the elbow. It'll heal, but not in time. Oh well, I'll probably be peaking in '88." She managed a brave smile.

"I'm sorry about that. Damn."

"Other than that, I'm okay. I have some bad dreams at night, and I get spooked easily. I still have a lot to work out. I'm gonna see somebody down here to talk to. Since I'm not going to LA, I'm going to spend the summer here with my folks."

"Listen, could you wind up my bed or something so I can see you better. This lying flat on my back makes it hard to talk."

"Sure. Here's your button. It'll do it automatically." She pressed it, and I moved toward a sitting position.

"That's fine. Thanks."

"Oh, by the way, that friend of yours, Arnie Kendall, showed up. I know what you mean about him. When he showed up I told him I didn't think I needed to be watched. He said if that's what you wanted, that was what he was here to do until you said otherwise. He was always around, kind of weird, but reassuring too. He's been outside your door since you were brought in. Chief Hungerford doesn't like him one bit or your other friend. The one Arnie called."

"Who else is here?"

"A guy named O'Neil. A lawyer. In fact, he said I should get him whenever you wake up. He wants to talk to you right away."

"Okay. Why don't you do that — and come back afterward. I'd like to talk some more with you."

"Sure thing." She patted my hand and got up to leave.

"Oh Wendy." She turned back to me. All expression was absent from her face, just like that moment before she began to approach her throw. "Thanks for being here when I woke up. There's nobody else I'd rather have seen." Her face assembled a radiant look of equal parts brilliant blue eyes and ear to ear grin.

"Be right back."

When she left, Arnie stuck his head in.

"You gonna live?" he asked without apparent interest.

"Yeah. I'm gonna live."

"Glad to hear it," he said. "By the way, you got lucky, very lucky." His tone was one of reproach but not rebuke.

I countered with, "You know what they say: I'd rather be lucky than good."

He was having none of it. "I know what the fools say. I say it's better to be lucky and good. You got careless. Rest up. We'll talk about it later.

"Oh, yeah — do you still want me to guard that lady?"

"No need. She killed the guy herself."

"Good for her."

I lay back to rest for a minute. "Arnie, thanks for coming down."

"You called, didn't you? Now rest up. I'll be around." With that, he closed the door.

Walt O'Neil is my lawyer. He is also my friend. Walt entered and crossed the room to with that jointless silken stride of his. He looked down solicitously at me and said, "Leo, me boy, you look a bit under the weather."

"Keen insight into the obvious, counselor. Now just how

bad a fix am I in that you wanted to see me right away upon awakening?"

"Leo, Leo, I'm injured. I wanted to see you right away to assure myself you were okay." Walt looked hurt.

"I'm sorry man. Thanks." I felt like a schmuck for having misjudged him.

"And to make sure my fee would be paid." He smiled at me. That smile was an invitation to consider myself forgiven. I took him up on it.

"As for your fix, I don't think it's real bad. Let me ask you some questions and then I want you to lie back, look exhausted, and let me do the talking."

"Be my guest. What do you want to know?"

"The girl, Sullivan, she says she killed Bascomb in self-defense. That he was killing you. Is that so?"

"Quite true."

"Very good. Now Saunders isn't talking to anyone about what happened on board that boat under advice of his counsel. If he were eventually to tell his tale, is there anything you did on board that vessel to place yourself in jeopardy?"

"Not a thing. I was a good boy." I was settling into the banter that was typical of our time together. It felt good to do so. One more aspect of the "life as usual" I so eagerly wished to reclaim.

"Are there any reasons you particularly want to tell anyone what happened out there? From what I have pieced together I can imagine you being 'spiritually aligned,' shall we say, with Saunders and might wish to protect him."

"A fair reading of things."

"So a position of silence with the authorities would be a course of action you would endorse?"

"By all means. Feel free to explain my silence all you want."

"So be it. Let's have a go round with Chief Hungerford."

Walt went to the door, opened it, and Chief Hungerford walked past him. They were a study in contrasts: The chief,

202 □ *BENJAMIN M. SCHUTZ*

short, rotund, bristling with indignation; Walt, long, lean, and languid.

The chief looked at Walt once with distaste and then at me. "Nice to see you're back with the living, Haggerty. I'll skip the amenities. I'd like to ask you some questions about the deaths of Bubba Bascomb and Justin Randolph."

Walt interrupted, "Excuse me, Chief, but may I ask a couple of questions?" Without waiting for a reply he went on. "First, my understanding is that if his story confirms Miss Sullivan's there would be no charges filed against her as it was self-defense, correct?"

"Yeah, that's correct."

"Fine. Tell him what happened, Leo."

I gave Hungerford a truncated version of events, omitting what I'd seen and heard in the house. As he listened, he shifted his weight from foot to foot, obviously anxious to move on. "Fine, fine. That fits her story to a T. I've got no interest in prosecuting that girl. Unofficially speaking, that bastard needed killing. I'm sure you'll provide us with a signed statement when we need one."

"Of course, Chief."

"Let's move on to the boat. What happened out there?"

Walt again stepped in. "Excuse me, Chief. In what capacity are you asking my client to answer?"

"What's that supposed to mean?" Hungerford snapped.

"Exactly what I said. Do you want the answer of a potential witness to a crime or of a dutiful citizen complying with a police request?"

"Hell, he's a witness. He was on the boat with them. They were picked up together."

"Quite true. He and Mr. Saunders were rescued together, but what crime was committed?"

"Quite a few, counselor. Assault and battery, kidnapping, murder."

"Oh? You have witnesses that put my client there at the time of these offenses?"

"No. Not yet."

"I see. You have recovered a body and the coroner's inquest yielded a finding of death at the hands of another?"

"No. Dammit. I don't have a body." Hungerford had taken off his hat and was spinning it on his forefinger.

"Have you found any witness to show that Mr. Saunders took Mr. Randolph out on that boat?"

"No. Not a one. Once the Magliotti killing was tied to Randolph, everyone went blind. Tony senior has a lot of friends in this town."

"So you don't have a crime even. Just a missing person. You'd like Mr. Haggerty to tell you if he knows anything about this missing person. Is that correct, Chief?"

Walt was pressing for all he could get. I felt bad for the chief. His adherence to his duty had saved Wendy's and my life. I wanted to help him, but I wanted to help Herb Saunders more. Walt started up again. "Mr. Saunders, I understand, has refused to answer any questions about the whereabouts of Justin Randolph. Is that correct?"

"Yeah." Hungerford had a defeated look. I was sure he wasn't pursuing this out of a love for Justin Randolph, but rather because the law was important to him. Everyone had to abide by it or face the consequences, regardless of his personal feelings. Law for all or there's law for none. We were abiding by the law, but not assisting it. Through that distinction justice slips in and out.

"I have advised my client that he has no legal obligation to answer your questions, but he has assured me that should it be determined that a crime was committed he will come back and assist the investigation in any way that he can. Isn't that right, Leo?"

"Absolutely."

"If that's all, Chief, my client is quite exhausted and needs his rest."

"I'll bet he does." Hungerford's voice was bitter.

"Chief, I'm sorry." That was all I could say. I was losing the respect of someone who had stuck his neck out for me and that felt like quite a loss, but better that than helping Herb Saunders go to jail. It was the lesser of two evils, and the best I could do.

Hungerford left, and Walt turned back to me. "Rest up, my boy. I'm going to kick around town with Arnie for a couple of days to watch this blow over. I'm at the Ramada Inn outside of town. Call when you're up to getting together. Oh, one last thing. Mrs. Saunders sends you her thanks and wants to talk to you when you're up. Be careful there. Don't say anything to her about what happened out on the boat. Got it?"

I nodded. As he let himself out, Wendy Sullivan came back in and sat by the side of the bed.

"So, what do you want to talk about?" She crossed her forearms on the railing of the bed and put her head on them.

"I want to talk about being friends. The war's over."

"Okay. How do we go about it?"

"I don't know. That's a good question. I don't think I have any female friends. Women have always been just lovers, either would-bes or have-beens. This is new to me. It would be too easy to turn this into one more go round of that."

"Oh, would it?" she said with mock indignation.

"I didn't mean it like that. It'd be too easy for me to want to do that."

She thought for a moment and then said, "I'll tell you what I think. I'm in no position to be anybody's lover right not. I don't just mean sexually, but I'm not ready to settle down with anybody. After all, I have a gold medal to win in '88, right?"

I grinned and felt relieved by what she was saying.

She went on. "Friends are people you have fun with; you like who they are. You trust them to be honest with you, to share your feelings with, to look out for you, right?"

"Right."

"Well, I think we've done okay on all those things except having fun. Let's try to have some fun together for starters."

"Good idea. What's your idea of fun?" I said.

"Throwing a javelin." She laughed.

"Super, I was going to offer to take you fishing, remember."

"Let's try something new. Do you like to dance?"

"This is true confessions time, friend. I'd like to, but I don't know how and haven't been able to bring myself to take lessons."

"I love to dance. Let me teach you. It's fun, and you won't have to be nervous, 'cause we're friends, right?"

"Right, friend."

On that optimistic note, I finally yielded myself up to my body's demand for rest and sank away into a sleep so deep even my dreams could not find me.